D0051671

HARLEQUIN
RECOMMENDED
Read!

THE BLACK SHEEP'S
INHERITANCE

DYNASTIES: THE LASSITERS

MAUREEN CHILD

USA TODAY BESTSELLING AUTHOR

 **HARLEQUIN**®

*Desire*

**Powerful heroes...scandalous secrets...
burning desires.**

AVAILABLE THIS MONTH

#2293 ONE GOOD COWBOY
Diamonds in the Rough
Catherine Mann

#2294 THE BLACK SHEEP'S INHERITANCE
Dynasties: The Lassiters
Maureen Child

#2295 HIS LOVER'S LITTLE SECRET
Billionaires and Babies
Andrea Laurence

#2296 A NOT-SO-INNOCENT SEDUCTION
The Kavanaghs of Silver Glen
Janice Maynard

#2297 WANTING WHAT SHE CAN'T HAVE
The Master Vintners
Yvonne Lindsay

#2298 ONCE PREGNANT, TWICE SHY
Red Garnier

 EAN

"J.D. was a bastard.

"What he did was terrible," Colleen said. "But he did it because he loved you."

"He betrayed me," Sage insisted.

"Can't you say J.D. did you a favor, too?"

"I'm not ready to thank him. But I can say that if he hadn't stuck his nose in, I might not be standing here with a woman who turns my blood to fire with a look."

"Sage..."

"I've been trying to stay away from you—"

"I know," she said. "Why?"

"Because I want you too much. You're in my blood, Colleen."

"You're in mine, too."

They kissed, but just as the kiss was spiraling out of control, Sage pulled back. "Damned if we're going to be together in an old cabin, then in an equipment shed. Today, we're going to try an actual *bed*. Come with me."

* * *

The Black Sheep's Inheritance is a Dynasties:
The Lassiters novel—

A Wyoming legacy of love, lies and redemption!

* * *

Dear Reader,

I'm back in another continuity and have to say I love writing these books. It's a collaborative effort, with all of the authors working together to make the stories come alive. And since writing is pretty much a solitary experience, it's a lot of fun to work with your friends.

In *The Black Sheep's Inheritance,* you'll meet Sage Lassiter and Colleen Falkner. These two were so much fun to write about. They each have their "issues," but when they come together, it's magic.

I really hope you enjoy the Dynasties: The Lassiters continuity and my contribution to the whole! Visit me on Facebook or follow me on Twitter to keep up-to-date on what's happening.

Until then, I wish you great books and many happy hours of reading!

Maureen

THE BLACK SHEEP'S
INHERITANCE

——

MAUREEN CHILD

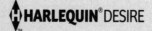

Special thanks and acknowledgment to Maureen Child for her contribution to the Dynasties: The Lassiters miniseries.

Recycling programs
for this product may
not exist in your area.

ISBN-13: 978-0-373-73307-1

THE BLACK SHEEP'S INHERITANCE

Copyright © 2014 by Harlequin Books S.A.

Printed in U.S.A.

Books by Maureen Child

Harlequin Desire

Silhouette Desire

Other titles by this author
available in ebook format.

MAUREEN CHILD

writes for the Harlequin Desire line and can't imagine a better job. Being able to indulge your love for romance, as well as being able to spin stories just the way you want them told is, in a word, perfect.

A seven-time finalist for the prestigious Romance Writers of America RITA® Award, Maureen is the author of more than one hundred romance novels. Her books regularly appear on the bestsellerlists and have won several awards, including a Prism, a National Readers' Choice Award, a Colorado Romance Writers Award of Excellence and a Golden Quill.

One of her books, *The Soul Collector,* was made into a CBS TV movie starring Melissa Gilbert, Bruce Greenwood and Ossie Davis. If you look closely, in the last five minutes of the movie, you'll spot Maureen, who was an extra in the last scene.

Maureen believes that laughter goes hand in hand with love, so her stories are always filled with humor. The many letters she receives assures her that her readers love to laugh as much as she does.

Maureen Child is a native Californian, but has recently moved to the mountains of Utah. She loves a new adventure, though the thought of having to deal with snow for the first time is a little intimidating.

To Stacy Boyd and Charles Griemsman, two editors
who make writing Desires such a terrific experience

One

The lawyer's office at the firm of Drake, Alcott and Whittaker was too crowded for Sage Lassiter's tastes. He much preferred being out on his ranch, in the cold, crisp air of a Wyoming spring. Still, he had no choice but to attend the reading of his adoptive father's will.

J.D. Lassiter had been dead only a couple of weeks and Sage was having a hard time coming to grips with it. Hell, he would have bet money that J.D. was far too stubborn to actually *die.* And now that he had, Sage was forced to live with the knowledge that now he would never have the chance to straighten things out between himself and the man who had raised him. Just like J.D. to go ahead and do something whether anyone else was ready for it or not. The old man had, once again, gotten the last word.

Sage couldn't have said when the tension between

him and J.D. had taken root, but he remembered it as an always-there kind of feeling. Nothing tangible. Nothing that he could point to and say: *There. That was it. The beginning of the end.* Instead, it was a slow disintegration of whatever might have been between them and it was beyond too late to think about it now. Old hurts, old resentments had no place in this room and nowhere to go even if he had let them take the forefront in his mind.

"You look like you want to hit something." His younger brother Dylan's voice came in a whisper.

Shooting him a hard look, Sage shook his head. "No, just can't really take in that we're here."

"I know." Dylan pushed his brown hair off his forehead and gave a quick look around the room before turning back to Sage. "Still can't quite believe J.D.'s gone."

"I was just thinking the same thing." He shifted, folded his arms across his chest and said, "I'm worried about Marlene."

Dylan followed his gaze.

Marlene Lassiter had stepped in as surrogate mother to Sage, Dylan and Angelica after Ellie Lassiter died during childbirth with Angie. She'd been married to J.D.'s brother Charles, and when she was widowed, she'd come home to Wyoming to live on Big Blue, the Lassiter ranch. She'd been nurturer, friend and trusted confidante for too many years to count.

"She'll be okay, eventually," Dylan said, then winced as they watched Marlene hold a sodden tissue to her mouth as if trying to stifle a wail of agony.

"Hope you're right," Sage muttered, uncomfortable seeing Marlene in pain and knowing there wasn't a damn thing he could do about it.

Marlene's son, Chance Lassiter, sat to one side of her,

his arm thrown protectively around her shoulders. He wore a leather jacket tossed on over a long-sleeved white shirt. Dark blue jeans and boots completed the outfit, and the gray Stetson he was never without was balanced on one knee. He was a cowboy down to his bones and the manager of J.D.'s thirty-thousand-acre ranch, Big Blue.

"You have any idea what the bequests are?" Dylan asked. "Couldn't get a thing out of Walter."

"Not surprising," Sage remarked with a sardonic twist of his lips. Walter Drake was not only J.D.'s lawyer, but practically his clone. Two more stubborn, secretive men he'd never met. Walter had made calls to all of them, simply telling them when and where to show up and not once hinting at what was in J.D.'s will. Logan Whittaker, another partner in the firm, was also working on J.D.'s will but he hadn't been any more forthcoming than Walter.

Sage wasn't expecting a damn thing for himself. And it wasn't as if he needed money. He'd built his own fortune, starting off in college by investing in one of his friends' brilliant ideas. When that paid off, he invested in other dreamers, and along the way he'd amassed millions. More than enough to make him completely independent of the Lassiter legacy. In fact, he was surprised he had been asked to be here at all. Long ago, he'd distanced himself from the Lassiters to make his own way, and he and J.D. hadn't exactly been close.

"Have you talked to Angelica since this all happened?" Dylan frowned and glanced to where their sister sat beside her fiancé, Evan McCain, her head on his shoulder.

"Not for long." Sage frowned, too, and thought about the sister he and Dylan loved so much. Her much-anticipated wedding had been postponed because of their father's death and who knew when it would happen now. Angelica's big brown eyes were red rimmed from crying and there were lavender shadows beneath those eyes that told Sage she wasn't sleeping much. "I went to see her a couple of days ago, hoping I could talk to her, but all she did was bawl." His scowl deepened. "Hate seeing her like that, but I don't know what the hell we can do for her."

"Not much really," Dylan agreed. "I saw her yesterday, but she didn't want to talk about what happened. Evan told me she's not sleeping, hardly eating. She's taking this really hard, Sage."

Nodding, he told his brother, "She and the old man were so close, of course she's taking it hard. Not to mention, J.D. collapsing at her rehearsal dinner adds a whole new level of misery. We've just got to make sure she gets past this. We'll tag team her. One of us going to see her at least every other day…"

"Oh," Dylan said, chuckling, "Evan will love having us around all the time."

"He's the one so hell-bent on marrying into the Lassiter family," Sage pointed out wryly. "If he takes one of us, he gets all of us. Best he figures that out now anyway."

"True." Dylan nodded then sat back in his chair. "Okay, then. We'll keep an eye on Angelica."

Dylan kept talking, now about his plans for the restaurant he was opening, but Sage had stopped listening. Instead, he watched Colleen Falkner, J.D.'s private nurse, slip quietly into the room, then make her way to the front, where she took a seat beside Marlene. The older woman gave her a watery smile of welcome and took her hand in a firm grip.

Sage narrowed his gaze on Colleen and felt a hard jolt of awareness leap to life inside him—just as it had the night of the rehearsal dinner. The same night J.D. died.

That night, he'd really *noticed* her for the first time. They'd met in passing of course, but on that particular night, there had been something different about her. Something that tugged at him. Maybe it had been seeing her long, amazing hair loose, cascading down her back in beautiful shimmering waves. Maybe it had been the short red dress and the black heels and the way they'd made her legs look a mile long. All he knew for sure was when he'd caught her eye from across the room, he'd felt a connection snap into place between them. He had started toward her, determined to talk to her—then J.D.'s heart attack had changed everything.

She wasn't wearing party clothes today, though. Instead, she wore baggy slacks, a sapphire-blue pullover sweater and her long, dark blond hair was pulled back into a braid that hung down between her shoulder blades. She had wide blue eyes that were bright with unshed tears and a full, rich mouth that tempted a man to taste it.

If he hadn't seen her in a figure-skimming red dress at the party—a dress that remained etched into his memory—Sage never would have guessed at the curves she kept so well hidden beneath her armor of wool and cotton.

He hadn't had much interaction with Colleen, since he and J.D. hadn't exactly been on the best of terms, so Sage didn't spend much time on Big Blue. But that night at the party, she'd intrigued him. Not only was she beautiful, but when J.D. collapsed, she had sprung into action, shouting orders like a general and taking charge until the paramedics showed up.

She had been devoted to J.D., had earned the family's affections—as evidenced by the way Marlene reached out to take the woman's hand—yet through it all had remained a bit of a mystery. Where was she from? Why had she taken a job working for a grumpy old man on a remote, if luxurious, ranch? And why the hell did he care?

"Colleen do something to you?"

He glanced at Dylan. "What?"

"Well, you're staring at her hard enough to set her hair on fire. What's up?"

Irritated to have been caught out, Sage muttered, "Shut up."

"Ah. Good answer." Dylan just smiled, shook his head and leaned forward to ask Chance something.

Sage let his gaze slide carefully back to Colleen. She bent her head to whisper something to Marlene, and he watched that long, silky braid slide across her shoulder, baring the nape of her neck. Soft blond curls brushed against her skin and he suddenly had the urge to touch her. To stroke that skin, to slide his fingers through her hair, to— He cut that thought off as fast as he could and scowled to himself.

The only possible reason she had for being here was if she was mentioned in J.D.'s will. Sure, J.D. had needed a nurse over his last few months, with his health failing, but such a beautiful one? Was that why she'd taken the job of caring for the old man? Had she been hoping for a nice payoff someday? Maybe he should spend a little time looking into Colleen Falkner, he thought. Do some checking. Make sure—

"You're looking at her again," Dylan pointed out.

Glaring at his brother and ignoring the smile on the man's face, Sage grumbled, "Don't you have something else to do?"

"Not at the moment."

"Lucky me."

"I just think it's interesting how fascinated you seem to be by Colleen."

"I'm not fascinated." *Much.* He shifted uncomfortably in his chair and told himself to stop thinking about her. How could the woman have gotten to him so easily? Hell, he hadn't even really *talked* to her.

"Not what it looks like from where I'm sitting."

"Then maybe you should sit somewhere else." He wasn't fascinated. He was…interested. Attracted. There was a difference.

Dylan laughed shortly. True to form, Sage's younger brother was almost impossible to insult. He was easygoing, charming and sometimes Sage thought his younger brother had gotten all the patience in the family. But he was also stubborn and once he got his teeth into something, he rarely let it go.

Like now, for example.

"She's single," Dylan said.

"Great."

"I'm just sayin'," his brother continued, "maybe you could leave your ranch once in a while. Have an actual date. Maybe with Colleen."

Sage drew his head back and stared at his brother. "Are you running a dating service I don't know about?"

"Fine," Dylan muttered, sitting back in his chair. "Have it your way. Be a hermit. End up becoming the weird old guy who lives alone on an isolated ranch."

"I'm not a hermit."

"Yeah? When's the last time you had a woman?"

Frowning, Sage said, "Not that it's any of your business, but I get plenty of women."

"One-night stands? Nice."

Sage preferred one-night stands. He didn't do commitment, and spending time with women who felt the same way avoided a lot of unnecessary hassle. If his brother wanted to look for more in his life, he was welcome to. As for Sage, he liked his life just the way it was. He came and went as he pleased. When he wanted a woman, he went and found one. When he wanted to be left the hell alone, he had that, too.

"Now that you mention it," he said quietly, "I haven't noticed you busy developing any serious relationships, either."

Dylan shrugged, folded his arms across his chest and said, "We're not talking about *me*."

"Yeah, well, we're done talking about *me,* too."

Then the office door opened, and lawyer Walter Drake stepped inside and announced, "All here?" He swept the room with a sharp-eyed gaze and nodded to himself. "Good. Then we can get started."

"I don't know if I'm ready for this," Dylan grumbled.

Sage was more than ready. He wanted this day done and finished so he could get back to his ranch.

After settling himself behind a wide oak desk, Walter, an older man who looked like the stereotypical image of an "old family retainer"—handsome, gray haired and impeccably dressed—picked up a stack of papers and straightened them unnecessarily. That shuffle of paper and the rattle of the window panes as a cold wind gusted against it were the only sounds in the room. It was as if everyone had taken a breath and held it.

Walter was clearly enjoying his moment in the spotlight. Every eye in the room was on him. Once again, his gaze moved over the people gathered there and when he finally came to Angelica, he gave her a sad, sympathetic smile before speaking to the room. "I know how hard this is on all of you, so I'll be as brief as possible."

Sage would be grateful.

"As you all know, J.D. and I knew each other for more than thirty years." Walter paused, smiled to himself and added, "He was a stubborn man, but a proud one, and I want you all to know that he took great care with his will. He remade it just a few months ago because he wanted to be sure to do the right thing by all of you."

Scraping one hand across his face, Sage shifted in the uncomfortable chair. He flicked a quick glance out the window and saw dark clouds rushing across the sky. *April in Wyoming,* he mused. It could be sunny in the morning and snowing by afternoon. And right now, it looked as though a storm was headed their way. Which only fed the urge to get back to his ranch before the bad weather hit.

"There are a lot of smaller provisions made to people J.D. thought well of over the years," Walter was saying. "I won't be reading them aloud today. Nor will I make mention of other estate business that will be handled separately."

Sage frowned thoughtfully and shifted his gaze to Walter. Handled separately? Why? What was the lawyer trying to hide? For that matter, what had *J.D.* been trying to hide? He braced his elbows on his thighs and leaned forward, keeping his gaze fixed on Walter as if the man was about to saw a woman in half. Or pull a dove from a magic hat.

"That part of the will is, at this time, not to be shared with the family."

"Why not?" Sage's question shattered the stillness left in the wake of Walter's startling statement.

The older man met Sage's gaze squarely. "Those were J.D.'s wishes."

"How do we know that?" An insulting question and he knew it, but Sage didn't stop himself. He didn't like secrets.

Dylan jammed his elbow into Sage's side, but he didn't so much as flinch. Just kept staring at the lawyer waiting for an answer.

"Because I tell you so," Walter said, stiffening in insult.

"C'mon, Sage," Dylan muttered. "Let it go for now."

He didn't want to, but he would. Only because Marlene had turned in her seat to give him a worried frown. Damned if he'd do anything to upset her any further than she already was. Nodding to the woman he thought of as a mother, he promised himself that he'd keep his silence for now, but that didn't mean this was the end of it.

"Now," Walter said firmly, "if that's settled, I'd like to continue. After all, the heart and soul of the will is what we're here to discuss today." He paused only long enough to smooth one hand across his neatly trimmed silver beard. "I appreciate you all coming in on such short notice, and I promise to get through this as quickly as possible."

Sage didn't know if the man was deliberately trying to pump up the suspense in the room or if he was just a naturally dramatic lawyer. But either way, it was working. Everyone there shifted uncomfortably in their seats as Walter read aloud the strange, coma-inducing legal phrases leading up to the actual bequests. One or two of those phrases resonated with Sage.

Sound in mind and body. Well, in mind, anyway, Sage told himself. J.D. had been sick for a while, but the old man's brain was as sharp the day he died as it was when he was nothing but a kid starting out. Which meant J.D. had had a reason for keeping these so-called secrets from the family even after his death. A flicker of anger bristled inside him, and Sage admitted silently that it sucked to be angry at a dead man, because you had no way of confronting him. J.D. was probably loving this, he thought. Even after he was gone, he was still running the show.

But as soon as he had the chance, Sage promised himself a long talk with J.D.'s lawyer.

"To my dear sister-in-law, Marlene…" Walter paused to smile at the woman in question. "I leave a ten-percent share in the Big Blue ranch along with ownership of the main ranch house for as long as she lives. I also leave her enough cash to maintain her lifestyle—" Walter broke off and added, "J.D. got tired of all the 'legal speak,' as he called it, and had me write the rest down just as he spoke it." He took a breath and continued, "Marlene, I want you to have some fun. Get on out there and enjoy your life. You're a good-looking woman and too damn young to fold up and die alone."

Marlene sniffed, then laughed shortly and mopped at her tears. The rest of the room chuckled with her, and even Sage had to smile. He could hear the old man's gruff voice as if he were there with them. J.D. and Marlene had been an unofficial couple for years. More than that though, Marlene had been a rock to three motherless young kids and to a man who had lost the love of his life.

"To Chance Lassiter, my nephew, I leave a sixty-percent share in Big Blue and enough cash to take some time and enjoy yourself a little." Walter paused and added, "The cash amounts mentioned in the will are specific and will be discussed privately with each of you at a later date."

Chance looked stunned and Sage was glad for him. The man loved that ranch and cared for it every bit as meticulously as J.D. had himself.

"You take care of Blue, Chance," Walter kept reading, "and she'll do the same for you."

"To Colleen Falkner," he went on and Sage shifted his gaze to the blonde. "I leave the sum of three million dollars."

Colleen gasped and rocked back in her chair. Blue eyes wide, mouth open, she stared at Walter as if he had two heads. If she was acting then send her an Oscar fast, Sage thought dryly. She looked as genuinely surprised as he was. J.D. had left three million dollars to his *nurse?*

Walter kept reading. "Colleen, you're a good girl and with this money, I want you to go on and chase your dream down. Don't wait until it's too late."

"Oh, my—" She shook her head in disbelief, but Walter was moving on already and Sage braced himself for whatever came next.

"To my son Dylan Lassiter, I leave controlling interest in Lassiter Grill Group, and enough cash to tide you over while you take it to the top. Oh, and I'm giving you ten-percent share of the Big Blue, too. It's your home, never forget that."

Beside Sage, Dylan looked shell-shocked and he

couldn't blame him. Hell, the man was now the owner of one of the fastest-growing restaurant groups in the country. If that didn't stop your heart a little, you weren't human.

"My son Sage Lassiter—"

Sage tensed for whatever was coming. He wouldn't have put it past J.D. to take one last swipe at him from the grave. To remind him publicly of the distance that had grown between them over the years. Like oil and water, Sage thought, he and J.D. had just never managed to mix well together.

"Sage," Walter read with a shake of his head, "you're my son and I love you. We butted heads too many times to count, but make no mistake, you're a Lassiter through and through. I'm leaving you twenty-five-percent interest in Lassiter Media, a ten-percent share in Big Blue— to remind you that's always your home—and lastly some cash that you won't want and don't need."

Surprised and touched, Sage snorted.

Walter continued word for word, "You're building your ranch your own damn way, just like I did. I admire that. So take this cash and buy something for that ranch. Something that will always remind you that your father loved you. Whether we could get along together or not."

Damn. The old man had surprised him one last time, was all Sage could think. His throat felt like a fist was squeezing, closing off his air. If he didn't get out of here soon, he was going to make a damn fool of himself. How the hell did J.D. know how to touch him, even from beyond the grave? How had he scripted words in a will months ago that could reach out long after he was gone to do what he hadn't been able to do in life?

"And lastly," Walter was saying, "I come to my beloved daughter, Angelica Lassiter. You are my heart and soul and the light of my life."

Sage glanced at his sister and saw her beautiful face crumple into tears again.

"And so," Walter read, "I leave you, Angelica, a ten-percent share of Big Blue, just like your brothers, the Lassiter estate in Beverly Hills, California, enough cash for you to spoil yourself some and finally, a ten-percent share in Lassiter Media."

"What?" Sage jumped to his feet, outraged, and Dylan was just a breath behind him. All of the warm feelings for his adoptive father vanished in a blink. How could he do that to Angelica? He'd groomed his daughter for years to take over the day-to-day operations of Lassiter Media, a conglomerate of radio, TV, newspapers and internet news outlets. Hell, she'd practically been running the damn thing on her own since J.D. got sick. And now he cut her out of the thing she loved?

"You can't be serious," Sage argued hotly, with a quick look at his sister's shocked, ashen features. "She's been running Lassiter Media for J.D. He left *me* more interest than Angie? That's insane!"

"We'll challenge the damn will," Dylan was saying, moving toward his sister to lay one hand on her shoulder in a show of solidarity.

"Damn straight," Sage agreed, glaring at the lawyer as if it were all his fault.

"There's more," Walter said, clearing his throat uncomfortably. "And I warn you, try to challenge this will and you might all be sorry—but more about that later. For now, voting control with forty-one-percent share of Lassiter Media, chairmanship and title of CEO, I leave to Evan McCain."

"Evan?" Angelica pulled away from her fiancé even as he was rising to his feet, stunned speechless.

"What the hell is going on here, Walter?" Sage demanded, coming around the corner of the man's desk to snatch up the will and read the terms himself.

"J.D. knew what he wanted to do and he did it," the lawyer argued.

"Well, it won't stand," Marlene said.

"Damn right it won't," Dylan piped up, charging the desk and snatching the will from his brother's grasp.

"It's not right." Chance came to his feet slowly, his calm, quiet voice nearly lost in the confusion.

"I can't believe it," Angelica murmured, looking at her fiancé as if she'd never seen him before.

"I swear I don't know anything about this," Evan said, taking a step toward her only to stop when she backed away from him.

"Well, somebody does, and I'm going to find out what's going on," Sage promised, then snapped his gaze to the door. Colleen Falkner was slipping out of the office like a damn ghost.

She'd gotten what she wanted, he told himself. He only wondered what she'd had to do for three million dollars. And he also had to ask himself if she'd known about J.D.'s plans. Had she been involved in his decision to rob Angelica of the very thing she cared most about?

Damned if he wouldn't find out.

Colleen leaned back against the door briefly, closing her eyes and forcing herself to drag a deep breath into her lungs. Her heart was pounding so hard and so fast she felt dizzy.

She hadn't expected anything like this.

Three million dollars?

Tears burned her eyes, but she frantically blinked them back. Now wasn't the time to indulge in tears for the loss of her friend—or for thinking about the future he had just made possible.

Behind her, she heard muffled shouts through the closed door. Sage Lassiter's voice was the most unmistakable. Though he didn't have to shout to be heard. The cold steel in his deep voice was enough to get the attention of anyone in the room.

God knew, he'd had *her* attention.

She'd felt him watching her earlier. Had sneaked a peek or two over her shoulder at him in return. He made her nervous. Always had. Which was why any time he'd come to the Big Blue ranch to visit his father—which wasn't often—Colleen had made herself scarce.

He was so…*male.*

Sage Lassiter was a force of nature. The kind of man women drooled over. And she was the kind of woman men like him never noticed. Well, not usually. He'd certainly noticed her today, though. And he hadn't looked very happy about it.

Tossing a quick look at the closed door behind her, Colleen hurried down the long beige hallway toward the elevators. She wanted to be long gone before Sage left that room.

Two

She made it as far as the parking lot.

"Colleen!"

Standing beside her car, Colleen took a breath and braced herself. That deep voice was unmistakable.

Goose bumps broke out on her arms and it wasn't because of the icy wind buffeting her. Blast Wyoming weather anyway. One day it was spring and the next, it was winter again. But the cold was the least of her worries.

It was him. Colleen had only been close to Sage Lassiter one time before today. The night of Angelica's rehearsal dinner. From across that crowded restaurant, she'd felt him watching her. The heat of his gaze had swamped her, sending ribbons of expectation unfurling throughout her body. He smiled and her stomach churned with swarms of butterflies. He headed toward her, and she told herself to be calm. Cool. But it hadn't worked. Nerves fired, knees weakened.

And just as he was close enough to her that she could see the gleam in his eyes, J.D. had his heart attack and everything had changed forever.

Looking back on that night, she told herself she was being silly even thinking that Sage might have been interested in her. He'd probably only wanted to ask her questions about his father's care. Or where the restrooms were.

In her own mind, she'd built up the memory of that night into something magical. But it was time to remember that she simply wasn't the kind of woman a man like him would ever notice. Sadly, that didn't stop *her* from noticing *him* and she hadn't been able to stop thinking about him since that night.

Now he was here, and she had to battle down a flurry of nerves. She turned and brushed a few stray, wind-blown hairs out of her face as she watched him approach.

Her heartbeat sped up at the picture he made. Sage Lassiter *stalked* across the parking lot toward her. It was the only word that could describe that long, determined stride. He was like a man on a mission. He wore dark jeans, boots and an expensively cut black sports jacket over a long-sleeved white shirt. His brown hair flew across his forehead and his blue eyes were narrowed against the wind. His long legs closed the distance between them in a few short seconds and then he was there. Right in front of her.

She had to tip her head back to meet his gaze and when she did, nerves skated down along her spine. For three months, she'd listened to J.D. Lassiter as he talked about his family. Thanks to those chats, she knew that

Sage was ruthless in business, quiet, hardheaded and determined to make his own way rather than capitalize on the Lassiter name. And though that last part had irritated J.D., she knew that he'd also admired Sage for it. How could he not? The older man had done the same thing when he was starting out.

Still, being face-to-face with the man who had filled her mind for weeks was a little unnerving. Maybe if she hadn't spent so much time daydreaming about him, she wouldn't feel so awkward right now. Colleen took another deep breath and held it for a moment, hoping to calm herself. But there was a flash of something she couldn't quite read in his eyes and the nerves won.

Wind slid down off the mountain, wrapped itself around them briefly then rushed on, delivering chills to the rest of Cheyenne. Ridiculously, Colleen was grateful for the cold wind. It was like a slap of common sense and though it wasn't enough to completely dampen her hormones, her next thought absolutely was.

The only reason she and Sage were here, about to talk, was because they had both attended the reading of his father's will. Remembering that helped her keep her voice steady as she gave him a smile and blurted, "I'm so sorry about your father."

A slight frown crossed his face briefly. "Thanks. Look, I wanted to talk to you—"

"You did?" There went her silly heart again, jumping into a gallop. He really was impossibly handsome, she thought absently—tall, dark and glower-y. There was an aura of undeniable strength that emanated from him. He was the kind of man other men envied and women wanted. Herself included. A brand-new flock of butterflies took off and flew in formation in the pit of her stomach. "You want to talk to me?"

"Yes," he said, his voice a deep rumble that seemed to roll across every one of her nerve endings. "I've got a couple questions…"

Fascination dissolved into truth. Instantly, Colleen gave herself a mental kick. Here she was, daydreaming about a gorgeous man suddenly paying attention to her when the reality was, he'd just lost his father. She knew all too well that the families left behind after a loss often had questions. Wanted to know how their loved one had been feeling. What they'd been thinking. And as J.D.'s private nurse, she had been with him the most during those final days.

And now that reality had jumped up to slap her, she was forced to acknowledge that Sage Lassiter had probably planned to talk to her the night of the party for the same reason. What had she been thinking? She'd half convinced herself that the rich, gorgeous Sage Lassiter was interested in *her*. God, what an idiot. Embarrassment tangled with a wash of disappointment before she fought past both sensations, allowing her natural empathy to come rushing to the surface.

"Of course you do." Instinctively, she reached out, laid her hand on his and felt a swift jolt of electricity jump from his body to hers. Totally unexpected, she felt the heat from that brief contact sizzle inside her. It was so strong, so real, she wouldn't have been surprised to actually *see* the arc of light shimmering between them. Quickly, she drew her hand back, then curled her fingers into her palm, determined to ignore the startling sensation.

His eyes narrowed further and she knew he'd felt it,

too. Frowning a little, he pushed one hand through his hair, fixed his gaze on hers and let her know immediately that whatever he might have felt, he was as determined as she to ignore it.

Shaking his head, he said, "No. I don't have any questions about J.D. Actually, *you're* the mystery here."

"Me?" Surprised, Colleen stared up at him, practically mesmerized by those cool blue eyes of his. "You think I'm a mystery? I'm really not."

"Oh, I don't know," he mused. "You went from nurse to millionaire in a few short months."

"What?" Confused now, she shook her head as if that might help clear things up a little. It didn't.

His lips curved but the smile didn't reach his eyes. "Sure, it's a big step, isn't it? I just wanted to say congratulations."

"Con—what? Oh. What?" Colleen's mind was slowly working its way past the hormonal surge she'd first felt when Sage had walked up to her. And now that she was able to think almost clearly again, it finally dawned on her what he was talking about. The bequest. The money J.D. had left her. He was making it sound…ugly.

Stung, she said quietly, "I don't know if *congratulations* is the right word."

"Why not?" He set one hand on the roof of her old, but completely reliable, Jeep and leaned in closer. "From private nurse to millionaire in one easy step. Not many people could have pulled that off."

Cold slithered through her and it was an icier feeling than anything the weather could provide. She glanced around the nearly empty parking lot. Only a half dozen or so cars were sprinkled around the area. The law office adjoining the lot seemed to loom over her, so for a second or two, she let her gaze drift past the city to the mountains in the distance. Sunlight glanced off the snow still covering the peaks. Gray clouds scudded across the deep blue sky and the ever-present wind tugged at her hair.

Just like always, the view of the mountains soothed her. She and her mother had moved to Cheyenne several years ago, and from the moment they arrived, Colleen had felt at home. She hadn't missed California and the beaches. It was the mountains that called to her. The wide-open spaces, the trees, the bite of cold in the air. In a moment, she was ready to face the man glaring at her. "I don't know what you mean."

But she did. She really did. His eyes were icy, detached and a muscle in his jaw ticked as if he were biting back all kinds of words he really wanted to say. J.D. had told her so much about Sage, and for the first time, she was seeing the less than pleasant aspects. *Ruthless. Hard.*

He was more different now from the man who had flirted with her from across a crowded room not two weeks ago than she would have thought possible. Did he really believe she had somehow engineered this bequest? That she'd tricked J.D. into leaving her money?

"I think you know exactly what I mean." His head tilted to one side as he studied her. "I just find it interesting that J.D. would bequeath three million dollars to a woman he didn't even know three months ago."

While she stood there, pinned in place by the sheer power of his gaze, Colleen felt like a bug on a glass slide under a microscope. The cold inside her began to melt beneath the steam of insult. She was still feeling a little shaky over J.D.'s death and the fact that he'd remembered her in his will. Now, staring up into Sage's eyes, seeing the flash of accusation gleaming there, she had to wonder if others would be thinking the same thing. What about the rest of the Lassiter family? Did they feel the same way? Would they also be looking at her with suspicion? Suddenly, she had a vision of not just the Lassiters but the whole town of Cheyenne whispering about her, gossiping.

That thought was chilling. She'd made Cheyenne her home and she didn't want her life destroyed by loose tongues spreading lies. Anger jumped to life inside her. She'd done nothing wrong. She'd helped an old man through his last days and she'd enjoyed his company, too. Since when was that a crime?

Gorgeous or not, Sage Lassiter had no right to imply that she'd somehow tricked J.D. into leaving her money in his will. Lifting her chin, she glared at him. "I didn't know he was going to do that."

"And you would have stopped him if you *had* known?"

The sarcasm in his tone only made the sense of insult deeper. She met his gaze squarely. On this, she could be completely honest. And she would keep being honest until people believed her. "I would have tried."

"Is that right?"

"Yes, it is," she snapped, and had the satisfaction of seeing surprise flicker in his eyes. "Whatever you might think of me, I'm very good at my job. And I don't ordinarily receive gifts from my patients."

"Really?" He snorted. "You consider three million dollars a *gift?*"

"What it represents was the gift," she countered, then

stopped herself. She didn't owe him an explanation and if she tried, he probably wouldn't accept it.

His features looked as if they'd been carved from marble. There was no emotion there, nothing to soften the harsh gaze that seemed to bore right through her as if he were trying to read everything she was.

Colleen fought past the temper still bubbling into a froth in the pit of her stomach and tried to remember that people grieved in different ways. He'd lost a father he'd been estranged from. There had to be conflicting emotions roiling inside him and maybe it was easier for Sage to lash out at a stranger than to deal with what he must be feeling at the moment. Though she knew from her many long talks with J.D. that he and his oldest son weren't close, Sage was clearly still dealing with a loss he hadn't been prepared for. That was bound to hit him hard and it was scarcely surprising that he wasn't acting rationally at the moment.

With that thought in mind, the tension inside her drained away. "You don't know me, so I can understand how you might feel that way. But what J.D. did was as big a shock to me as it was to you."

A long second or two ticked past as he watched her through those deep blue eyes of his. She couldn't help wondering what he was thinking, but his features gave her no clue at all. Seconds ticked past as the wind blew, the sky grew darker and the silence between them stretched taut. Finally, he straightened up and away from the car, shoved both hands into his pockets and allowed, "Maybe I was a little harsh."

She gave him a tentative smile that wasn't returned. Despite his words, he wasn't really bending. Sighing, she said, "A little. But it's understandable, considering what you're going through. I mean…I understand."

"Do you?" Still watching her, though the ice in his eyes had melted a bit.

"When my father died," she said, sliding back into her own memories, "it was horrible, despite the fact that we knew for months that it was coming. Even when death is expected, it's somehow a surprise when it actually happens. It's as if the universe has played a dirty trick on you. I was so angry, so sorry to lose him—I needed someone to blame." She paused and met his gaze. "We all do."

He snorted. "A nurse *and* a psychologist?"

She flushed. "No, I just meant…"

"I know what you meant," he said shortly, effectively shutting her down before she could offer more sympathy he clearly didn't want.

And just like that, the ice was back in his eyes. Then he glanced over his shoulder, noted that his family was walking out of the office building behind them and turned back to her. "I have to go."

She looked to where Marlene and Angelica were holding onto each other while Chance, Dylan and Evan squared off, obviously arguing. "Of course."

"But I'd like to talk to you again," he said, catching her by surprise.

"Sure, I—"

"About J.D.," he added.

A tiny flicker of something lovely disappeared in a wash of sympathy. Of course he wanted to talk to her about his father. He wanted to hear from the woman who had spent the most time with him in his last several months. Ridiculous to have ever thought that he might be interested in *her*. Sage Lassiter dated women who were socialites or celebrities. Why on earth would he ever be attracted to a private nurse who didn't even own a bottle of nail polish?

"Sure," she said, giving him another smile that went unreturned. "Anytime."

He nodded, then turned and strode across the parking lot toward his family.

Alone in the quickening wind, Colleen threw one look up at the sky and realized that a storm was coming.

"What was he *thinking?*" Dylan took a sip of his beer and set the bottle back onto the table. "Cutting Angie out like that? Dad had been grooming her for years to take over Lassiter Media."

They were at a small bar on the edge of the city. Marlene had taken Angelica off for a spa day, hoping to relax her. Evan had gone back to the office and Chance was at the ranch. Left to their own devices, Sage and Dylan had opted for drinks, and the chance to talk things over, just the two of them.

The customers here were locals, mostly cowboys, ranch hands and a few cops and firemen. It was a comfortable place that didn't bother trying to be trendy. The owner didn't care about attracting tourists. He just wanted to keep his regulars happy.

So the music was loud and country, blasting from a jukebox that was older than Sage. The floorboards were scarred from wooden chairs scraping across them for the past fifty years. The bar top gleamed and the rows of bottles behind the bar were reflected in a mirror that also displayed the image of the TV playing on the opposite wall. People came here to have a quiet drink. They weren't looking to pose for pictures or listen to tourists talking excitedly about "the Old West." This was modern-day Cheyenne, yet Sage had the feeling quite a few people rode into town half expecting stagecoaches and more than just the staged gunfights in the streets.

"I don't know," Sage muttered, unnecessarily answering his brother's rhetorical question.

Dylan kept talking, but Sage wasn't really listening. Instead he was remembering the look in Colleen's eyes when he'd confronted her in the parking lot. He'd wanted to talk to her. To see what she knew. To find out if she'd had any idea what J.D. had been up to.

Instead, he'd put her on the defensive right from the jump. He hadn't meant to just launch into an attack. But with the memory of his sister's tears still fresh in his mind, he'd snapped at Colleen.

Scrubbing one hand across his face, he realized that he was going to have to use a completely different tactic the next time he talked to her. And there *would* be a next time. Not only did she intrigue him on a personal level but there were too many questions left unanswered. Had she swayed J.D. into leaving her the money? Did she know why Angelica had lost everything? Did she maybe know something that might help him invalidate the will? His brain was racing.

"Angie was looking at Evan like he was the enemy instead of the man she loves."

"Hard not to," Sage said, mentally dragging himself back to the conversation at hand. "In one swipe, Evan took everything Angie thought was hers."

"Well, it's not like he stole it or anything," Dylan told him. "J.D. *left* it to him."

"Yeah," he grumbled. "J.D. was just full of surprises,

wasn't he? Still, doesn't matter how it happened. Bottom line's the same. Angie's out and Evan's in. Not surprising that she's angry at him."

"True." Dylan picked up his beer for another sip, then held the bottle, rubbing his thumb over the label.

"It was always tricky, the two of them engaged and working for the same company. But now that Angie's not even the boss anymore?" Sage shook his head grimly. "I just hope this will doesn't cause a breakup."

"Worst part is, I don't know what we can do about it. From the little Walter said, I don't think we'll be able to contest the will without everyone losing."

"That's Walter's opinion. We need to check into that with an impartial lawyer."

"If there is such a beast," Dylan muttered.

"I know." Sage lifted his glass and took a slow sip of very old scotch. The heat swarmed through his system, yet did nothing to ease the tight knot in the pit of his stomach.

His sister had been crushed by their father's will. His aunt Marlene was happy with her bequest but naturally worried for Angie. Chance was good, of course. Big Blue ranch was his heart and soul. Evan had looked as though he'd been hit in the head with a two-by-four, but once the shock eased, Sage couldn't imagine the man complaining about the inheritance. Except for how it was affecting Angie.

There was going to be tension between Evan and her. But Sage hoped to hell they could work it out and find their way past all of this. But for now, their wedding was still postponed and after the will reading, Sage had no idea how long that postponement was going to last.

As for himself, Sage was still staggered by his bequest from J.D. Hell, he'd gotten a bigger share of Lassiter Media than Angie had—and that just wasn't right. Every time he thought about this, he came back to one question: What the hell had J.D. been thinking? And the only way he had even the slightest chance of figuring that out was by getting close to Colleen.

She was the one who had spent the most time with J.D. in the past few months. Sage had heard enough about the young, upbeat, efficient nurse from Marlene and Angie to know that she had become J.D.'s sounding board. He'd talked to her more than he had to anyone else in the last months of his life. And maybe that was because it was easier to talk about your problems to a stranger than it was to family.

But then, J.D. had always been so damned self-sufficient, he'd never seemed to need anyone around him. Until he got sick. That was the one thing he and Sage had always shared in common—the need to go it alone. Maybe that was why they'd never really gotten close. Both of them were too closed off. Too wrapped up in their own worlds to bother checking in with others.

He scowled at the thought. Funny, he'd never before considered just how much he and his adoptive father were alike. Went against the grain admitting it now, because Sage had spent so much of his life rebelling against J.D.

Yes, he knew that Colleen was the one person who might help him make sense of all this. But he hadn't been prepared for that spark of something hot and undeniable that had leaped up between them when she touched him. Sure, he had been interested in her the night of the rehearsal dinner—a beautiful woman, alone, looking uncomfortable in the crowd. But he hadn't had a chance to talk to her, let alone touch her, before everything had changed in an instant. Now he thought again of that flash of heat, the surprise in her eyes, during their confrontation a little while ago, and had to force himself to shove the memory aside. It was clear just by looking at her that she wasn't a one-night-stand kind of woman—but that could change, he assured himself. He couldn't get the image of her out of his mind. Her wide blue eyes. The sweep of dark blond hair. A soft smile curving a full mouth that tempted a man. His body tightened in response to his thoughts. The attraction between them was hot and strong enough that he couldn't simply ignore it.

"So what were you talking to Colleen about?"

"What?" He snapped his gaze up to meet Dylan's, shoving unsettling thoughts aside. "I…uh…" Uncomfortable with the memory of his botched attempt at getting close to the woman, Sage scrubbed one hand across the back of his neck.

"I know that look," his brother said. "What did you do?"

"Might have gotten off on the wrong foot," he admitted, remembering the look of shock on Colleen's face when he'd practically accused her of stealing from J.D. Was she innocent? Or a good actress?

"Why'd you hunt her down in the first place?"

"Damn it, Dylan," he said, leaning across the table and lowering his voice just to be sure no one could overhear them. "She's got to know something. She spent the most time with J.D. Hell, he left her three million dollars."

"And?"

"And," he admitted, "I want to know what she knows. Maybe there's something there. Maybe J.D. bounced ideas off of her and she knew about the changes to the will."

"And maybe it'll snow in this bar." Dylan shook his head. "You know as well as I do that J.D. was never influenced by anyone in his life. Hell," he added with a short laugh, "you're so much like him in that it's ridiculous. J.D. made up his own mind, right or wrong. No way did his *nurse* have any information that we don't."

He had to admit, at least to himself, that Dylan had a point. But that wasn't taking into consideration that the old man had known he was getting up there in years and he hadn't been feeling well. Maybe he started thinking about the pearly gates and what he should do before he went. That had to change things. If it did, who better to share things with than your nurse?

No, Sage told himself, he couldn't risk thinking Dylan was right. He had to know for sure if Colleen Falkner knew more than she was saying. "I'm not letting this go, Dylan. But it's going to be harder to talk to her now, though, since I probably offended the hell out of her when I suggested that maybe she'd tricked J.D. into leaving her that much money."

"You *what?*" Dylan just stared at him, then shook his head. "Have you ever known our father to be tricked into *anything?*"

"No."

Still shaking his head, Dylan demanded, "Does Colleen seem like the deadly femme fatale type to you?"

"No," he admitted grudgingly. At least she hadn't today, bundled up in baggy slacks and a pullover sweater. But he remembered what she'd looked like the night of the party. When her amazing curves had been on display in a red dress that practically screamed *look at me!*

"You've been out on your ranch too long," Dylan was saying. "That's the only explanation."

"What's that got to do with anything?"

"You used to know how to charm people. Especially *women.* Hell, you were the king of schmooze back in the day."

"I think you're thinking of yourself. Not me," Sage said with a half smile. "I don't like people, remember?"

"You used to," Dylan pointed out. "Before you bought that ranch and turned yourself into a yeti."

"Now I'm Sasquatch?" Sage laughed shortly and sipped at his scotch.

"Exactly right," Dylan told him. "You're practically a legend to your own family. You're never around. You spend more time with your horses than you do people. You're a damn hermit, Sage. You never come off the mountain if you don't have to, and the only people you talk to are the ones who work for you."

"I'm here now."

"Yeah, and it took Dad's *death* to get you here."

He didn't like admitting, even to himself, that his brother was right. But being in the city wasn't something he enjoyed. Oh, he'd come in occasionally to meet a woman, take her to dinner, then finish the evening at her place. But the ranch was where he lived. Where he most wanted to be.

He shifted in his chair, glanced uneasily around the room, then slid his gaze back to his brother's. "I'm not a hermit. I just like being on the ranch. I never was much for the city life that you love so much."

"Well, maybe if you spent more time with people instead of those horses you're so nuts about, you'd have done a better job of talking to Colleen."

"Yeah, all right. You have a point." Shaking his head, he idly spun the tumbler of scotch on the tabletop. He studied the flash of the overhead lights in the amber liquid as if he could find the answers he needed. Finally, he lifted his gaze to his brother's and said, "Swear to God, don't know why I started in on her like that."

Dylan snorted, picked up his beer and took a drink. "Let's hear it."

So he told his brother everything he'd said and how Colleen had reacted. Reliving it didn't make him feel any better.

When he was finished, a couple of seconds ticked past before Dylan whistled and took another sip of his beer. "Man, anybody else probably would have punched you for all of that. I know I would have. Lucky for you Colleen's so damn nice."

"Is she?"

"Marlene loves her," Dylan pointed out. "Angie thinks she's great. Heck, even Chance has had nothing but good things to say about her, and you know he doesn't hand out compliments easy."

"All true," Sage agreed.

And yet…Sage's instincts told him she was exactly what she appeared to be. A private nurse with a tantalizing smile and blue eyes the color of a lake in summer. But he couldn't overlook what had happened. What J.D. had done in his will. And the only person around who might have influenced the old man was the one woman who had spent the most time with him. He had to know. Had to find out what, if anything, she knew about the changes to J.D.'s will.

And if she had had something to do with any of this, he would find a way to make her pay.

Three

The Big Blue ranch seemed empty without the larger-than-life presence of J.D. Lassiter. Colleen glanced out the window of the bedroom that had been hers for the past several weeks and smiled sadly. She was going to miss this place almost as much as she would miss J.D. himself.

But it was always like this for her, she thought sadly. As a private nurse, she slipped into the fabric of families—sometimes at their darkest hours. And when her job was done, she left, moving on to the next client. The next family.

She tugged on the zipper of her suitcase, flipped the lid open and then sighed. Colleen hated this part of her assignments. The packing up of all her things, the saying goodbye to another chapter in her life. Positioning these memories onto a high shelf at the back of her mind, where they could be looked at later but would be out of the way, making room for the next patient.

Only this time…maybe there wouldn't be another family.

She shook her head and realized that the silence of the big house was pressing down on her. The only other people at Big Blue right now were the housekeeper and the cook, and it was as if the big house was…lonely. It wouldn't be for long, though. Soon, Marlene, Angelica and Chance would be returning, and she wanted to be gone before they got home. They didn't need her here anymore. By rights, she should have left two weeks ago after J.D.'s death, but she'd stayed on at Marlene's request, to help them all through this hard time.

Colleen walked to the closet and gathered an armful of clothes, carrying them back to the bed. On autopilot, she folded and then stacked her clothing neatly in the suitcase and then went back for more. It wouldn't take long to empty the closet and the dresser she had been using. She'd only brought a few things with her when she moved into the guest room.

Normally, she didn't live in when she took a private client. But J.D. had wanted her close by and had been willing to pay for the extra care, to spare his family having to meet all of his needs. In the past couple of months, Colleen had grown to love this place. The ranch house was big, elegant and yet still so cozy that it wasn't hard to remember that it was, at its heart, a family home.

At that thought, Sage crept back into her mind. He, his brother and sister had all grown up here on this ranch, and if she listened hard enough, she was willing to bet she would be able to hear the long-silent echoes of children playing.

And strange, wasn't it, how her mind continually drifted back to thoughts of Sage? To be honest, he had been on her mind since the rehearsal dinner. He starred nightly in her dreams and even his coldly furious outburst that morning hadn't changed anything. In fact, it had only made her like him more. That outburst had shown her just how much he had cared for his father, despite their estrangement. And the sympathy she felt for the loss he'd suffered was enough to color his accusations in a softer light.

Her brief conversation with Sage Lassiter had left Colleen more shaken than the news that she was now a millionaire. Maybe because the thought of so much money was so foreign to her that her brain simply couldn't process it. But having the man of her dreams actually speak to her was so startling, she couldn't seem to think of anything but him. Even though he'd insulted her.

"Not his fault," she assured herself again as she folded her clothes and stuffed them into the suitcase. "Of course he'd be suspicious. He doesn't know me. He just lost his father. Why should he trust me?"

All very logical.

And yet the sting of his words still resonated with her. Because she couldn't get past the thought that everyone else would believe what he'd blurted out. That somehow she had tricked a sick old man into leaving her money. Maybe she *should* turn it down. Go back to the lawyer, tell him to donate the money to charity or something.

Releasing a breath, she stopped packing and lifted her gaze to the window of the room that had been home for the past three months. The view outside was mesmerizing, as always.

There were no curtains on the windows at Big Blue.

In the many talks Colleen and J.D. had had, she'd learned that was a decree from J.D.'s late wife, Ellie. She'd wanted nothing to stand between her and the amazing sweep of sky. There were trees, too—all kinds of trees. Pines, oaks, maples, aspen. There was a silence in the forest that was almost breathtaking. She loved being here in the mountains and wasn't looking forward to going back to her small condo in a suburb of Cheyenne.

But, a tantalizing voice in her mind whispered, *with your inheritance, you could buy a small place somewhere out here. Away from crowds. Where you could have a garden and trees of your own and even a dog.* A dog. She'd wanted one for years. But she hadn't gotten one because first, her father had been sick, and then when she and her mother moved to Cheyenne, they'd lived in apartments or condos. It hadn't seemed fair to her to leave an animal cooped up all day while she and her mom were at work.

Now, though…her mind tempted her with the possibilities that had opened up to her because of J.D. She could quit her job, focus on getting her nurse practitioner's license and start living the dream that had been fueling her for years. More than that, she could help her mom, make her life easier for a change. That thought simmered in her mind, conjuring up images that made her smile in spite of everything.

The winters in Cheyenne were beginning to get to Colleen's mother. Laura Falkner was always talking about moving to Florida to live with her widowed sister and maybe the two of them taking cruises together. Seeing the world before she was too old to enjoy it all.

With this inheritance, Colleen could make not only her own dreams come true, but her mother's, as well.

Her hands fisted on the blue cotton T-shirt she held. Should she take the money as the gift it had been meant to be? Or should she reject it because she was afraid what small-minded people might say?

"Wouldn't that be like a slap in the face to J.D.?" she asked aloud, not really expecting an answer.

"Lots of people wanted to slap J.D. over the years."

She whirled around to face Sage, who stood in the open doorway, one shoulder braced against the door-jamb. He leaned there casually, looking taller and stronger and somehow more intimidating than he had in the parking lot. And that was saying something. His cool blue gaze was locked on hers and Colleen felt the slam of that stare from all the way across the room.

Her heartbeat jumped into a gallop, her mind went blessedly blank for a second or two and her mouth dried up completely. There was a buzzing sensation going on inside her, too, and it was tingling long-comatose parts of her body back into life. What was it about this man that could turn her into such a hormonal wreck just by showing up?

"What? I mean," she muttered, irritated that once again she felt tongue-tied around him. She'd always thought of herself as a simple, forthright kind of woman. Before now, she had never had trouble talking to anyone. But all Sage had to do was show up and her mouth was so busy thinking of doing other more interesting things that it couldn't seem to talk. "I didn't know you were there."

"Yeah," he said, pushing away from the wall and strolling confidently into the room. "You seemed a little…distracted." He glanced around the sumptuous room, taking in the pale blue quilt, the dozen or more pillows stacked against a gleaming brass headboard and the brightly colored throw rugs covering the polished wood floor. "This place has changed some."

"It's a lovely room," she said, again feeling a pang about leaving.

He glanced at her and shrugged. "When I was a kid, this was my room."

His room. Oh, my. A rush of heat swept through her system so completely, she felt as if she'd gotten a sudden fever. She'd been living in Sage's room for the past few months. If she'd known that before, she might not have been able to sleep at all.

She smiled hesitantly. "I'm guessing it looks a lot different to you, then."

"It does." He walked to the window, looked out, and then turned back to her with a quick grin. "The trellis is still there, though. You ever climb down it in the middle of the night?"

"No, but you did?"

"As often as possible," he admitted. "Especially when I was a teenager. J.D. and I..." His voice trailed off. Then he cleared his throat and said, "Sometimes I just needed to get out of the house for a while."

Colleen tried to imagine Sage as an unhappy boy, escaping out a window to claim some independence. But with the image of the strong, dynamic man he was now, standing right in front of her, it wasn't easy.

"So," he said abruptly, "what do you want to slap J.D. for?"

The sudden shift in conversation threw her for a second until she remembered that he'd been listening when she was talking to herself.

"I don't. I mean…" She blew out a breath and said, "It's nothing."

"Didn't sound like nothing to me," he mused, turning his back on the window and the view beyond to look at her again.

Backlit against the window, he looked more broad shouldered, more powerful…just, *more.* The bedroom suddenly seemed way smaller than it had just a few minutes ago, too. Sage Lassiter was the kind of man who overtook a room once he was in it, making everyone and everything somehow diminished just with his presence. A little intimidating. And if she was going to be honest with herself, a *lot* exciting.

Which wasn't helping her breathing any. "I was thinking out loud, that's all."

"About?"

She met his gaze. "If you must know, about whether or not I should accept the money J.D. left me."

Surprise shone briefly in his eyes. "And the decision is?"

"I haven't made one yet," she admitted, dropping the T-shirt onto her half-packed suitcase. "To be honest, I don't know what I should do."

"Most people would just take the three million and run."

Colleen shrugged helplessly. "I'm not most people."

"I'm beginning to get that," he said, stuffing both hands into his jeans pockets as he walked toward her. "Look, I came on a little strong earlier—"

"Really?" She smiled and shook her head. She remembered everything he'd said that morning. Every word. Every tone. Every glittering accusation he'd shot at her from his eyes. She also remembered that electrical jolt she'd gotten when she touched him.

He nodded. "You're right. And I was wrong. J.D. wanted you to have the money. You should take it."

"Just like that?" She studied him, hoping to see some tangible sign of why he'd changed his mind, but she couldn't read a darn thing on his face. The man was inscrutable. As a businessman, the ability to blank out all expression had probably helped him amass his fortune. But in a one-on-one situation, it was extremely annoying.

"Why not?" He moved even closer and Colleen could have sworn she felt actual *heat* radiating from his body to enclose her in a cocoon of warmth. Warmth that spread to every corner of her body. She swallowed hard, lifted her chin and met his eyes when he continued. "Colleen, if you're thinking about turning down your inheritance because of what I said, then don't."

A cold breeze slipped beneath the partially open window and dissipated the warmth stealing through her. That was probably a good thing. "I admit, what you said has a lot to do with my decision. But mostly, I'm worried that other people might think the same thing."

He pulled one hand from his pocket and slapped it down on the brass foot rail. "And that would bother you?"

Stunned, she said, "Of course it would bother me. It's not *true*."

"Then what do you care what anyone else thinks?"

Did he really not see what it would be like? Were the rich really so different from everyone else? "You probably don't understand because you're used to people talking about you. I mean, the Lassiters are always in the papers for something or other."

"True," he acknowledged.

"And as for you, the press loves following you around. They're always printing stories about the black sheep billionaire." She stopped abruptly when she caught his sudden frown. "I'm sorry, it's just—"

"You seem to keep up with reports about me," he said softly.

"It's hard not to," she lied, not wanting him to know that she really did look for stories about him in the paper and magazines—not to mention online. God, she was practically a stalker! "The Lassiter family is big news in Cheyenne." She covered for herself nicely. "The local papers are always reporting about you and your family."

He snorted. "Yeah, and I'm guessing the will is going to be front-page news as soon as someone leaks the details."

Surprised, she asked, "Who would do that?"

"Any number of clerks in the law offices, I should think," he said. "The right amount of money and people will do or say anything."

"Wow…that's cynical."

"Just a dose of reality," he said, his hand tightening around the brass rail until his knuckles whitened. "I used to think most people were loyal, with a sense of integrity. Then I found out differently."

"What happened?" she asked, caught up in the glimmer of old pain and distant memories glittering in his eyes. The house was quiet, sunlight drifting in through the bedroom window, and it felt as though they were the only two people on the planet. Maybe that's why she overstepped. Maybe that's why she allowed herself to wonder about him aloud rather than just in her mind.

He almost looked as though he would tell her, then in an instant, the moment was gone. His features were once again schooled in pokerlike stillness and his eyes were shuttered. "Doesn't matter. The point is, you shouldn't let gossips rule your decisions."

Colleen was sorry their all-too-brief closeness was gone, but it was just as well. "It sounds so simple when you say it like that, but I don't like being gossiped about."

"Neither do I," he said, glancing down at her suitcase, then lifting his gaze to hers again. "Doesn't mean I can stop it."

He was right and she knew it. Still, he was a Lassiter and rumors and prying questions came with the territory. She was a nobody and she preferred it that way. "Maybe if I don't accept the inheritance, they won't bother because there would be nothing to talk about."

He smiled, but it wasn't a comforting expression. "Colleen, people are going to gossip. Whether you take the money or not, people will talk. Besides, trust me, a beautiful woman like you taking care of J.D. all these months...there's gossip already."

Beautiful? He thought she was *beautiful?* Then what he said struck home. A flush of embarrassment washed over her as she realized he was probably right. There was no doubt talk already, and with her living here at the ranch, she had fed the flames of the gossip.

"That's just awful. I was his *nurse.*"

"A young, pretty nurse with a sick old man. Doesn't take much more than that to get tongues wagging."

She argued that because she had to. For her own peace of mind. Colleen hated to think that people were making ugly accusations about a sweet old man. And oh, God, had her *mother* heard the talk? No. If she had, she would have said something, wouldn't she?

Shaking her head, Colleen said, "But J.D. wasn't my first patient. This has never happened to me before."

He shrugged the argument aside. "You'd never worked for a Lassiter before, either. I'm only surprised you haven't already heard the speculation."

She plopped down onto the edge of her mattress, her mind racing as images from the past few months flashed across her brain. She hadn't really paid attention before, but now that she was looking at things in a new light, she realized he was right. The gossip had already started. She remembered knowing winks, slow smiles and whispered conversations cut short when she entered any of the local shops.

"Oh, my God. They really think that I—that J.D.— oh, this is humiliating."

"Only if you let them win," he said quietly and she looked up at him, waiting for him to continue. "Small minds are always looking for something to occupy them. If you live your life worried about what they're saying, you won't do anything. Then they win."

"I really hate this," she murmured. He did have a point, but this was the first time in her life that she was the subject of gossip. She'd led a fairly quiet existence until she'd taken the job with J.D.

Sage was looking at this from an entirely different angle. The truth was, as a Lassiter, he was insulated from the nastiest rumors and innuendos. He didn't have to worry about what people were saying about him, because his career was already made, and he had a powerful fam-

ily name behind him. Besides, how bad was it to have
people discussing how incredibly gorgeous you were?

No, this was different. If people were talking about
her, it could affect her work. Her life. If the nursing
agency she worked for got wind of any of this, they
might be reluctant to send her out on other assignments—and that made her cringe. On the other hand,
if she simply accepted J.D.'s generosity, she could make
her own way. Though she would still, as a nurse practitioner, have to work through local doctors and hospitals.

"My head hurts," she muttered.

He laughed and it was such a rich, surprising sound,
it startled her. Looking up at him, she saw that his eyes
were shining and the wide smile on his face displayed a
dimple she was fairly certain didn't show up very often.

"You're thinking about this too much."

"It's very hard not to," she told him, shaking her head.
"I've never been in this position before and I'm not really sure what to do about it."

"Do what you want to do," he advised.

Want was a big word. She *wanted* a lot of things.
World peace. Calorie-free chocolate. Smaller feet. Her
gaze drifted to Sage's mouth and locked there. And she
really wanted to kiss him.

As that thought settled into the forefront of her mind,
Colleen cleared her throat and tried for heaven's sake to
get a grip. Honestly, she'd been alone so long, was it really so surprising that a man like Sage Lassiter would
tangle her up into knots without even trying?

"Everything okay?" He was frowning now.

"Fine. Fine." She breathed deeply and repeated,
"What I want. Do what I want."

"Not so hard, is it?"

"You wouldn't think so..." But she'd been raised to consider more than her wants. There was doing the right thing, and in this case, she just didn't know what that was.

"You know," he murmured, "once you show people you don't care what they think, they usually stop talking about you."

Wryly, she asked, "And if you *do* care what they're saying?"

His lips quirked into a quick half smile that tugged at something inside her. "Well, that's a different story, isn't it? But why would you care?"

"Because I have to work here. Live here. If people think—" She swallowed hard. Everything she'd worked toward, everything she'd built in the past five years. Her reputation...her hopes and dreams. It could all disappear.

Suddenly, the windfall from J.D. looked like more of a curse than a blessing.

"You're giving other people all the power here," Sage said, drawing her attention away from her thoughts.

"I don't want to, but..." Shaking her head, she folded her hands together on her lap. "Ever since this morning, my mind's been filled with questions. And now I don't know what to do about this."

"Not much you can do about it." Sage walked around her, pushed the open suitcase out of his way and took a seat beside her on the bed. "The will's a done deal."

"But I could donate the money."

He shrugged. "People would still talk. The only difference would be you wouldn't have the money."

She sighed heavily and turned to look at him. He was so close to her, his muscular thigh was just a bare inch from brushing against hers. Heat rushed through her and

Colleen forced a deep breath as she met his gaze. His eyes weren't as frosty as they had been earlier, yet they were still unreadable. As if he'd drawn shutters down, to keep others from sensing his emotions. He was so closed off—much like J.D. had been when she'd first come to take care of him. But, she reminded herself, it hadn't taken her long to bypass the older man's defenses and get him to really talk to her.

The difference was, Sage wasn't her patient. He was a strong, completely masculine male who made her feel things she hadn't felt in far too long. Which was, of course, not only ridiculous, but inappropriate. He was the son of her patient. A family member who'd just gone through a devastating loss. He wasn't interested in her and she would only do herself a favor if she found a way to tamp down the rush of attraction she felt every time he came close. Of course, *way* easier said than done.

"Look," he said, his voice quiet, "why don't we have dinner tonight? Give us a chance to talk some more."

She blinked at him, so stunned she could hardly manage to croak, "You're asking me out?"

One corner of his mouth lifted. "I'm asking you to have dinner with me."

Not a date. Of course it wasn't a date. Idiot.

"Why?" *And why are you questioning it,* her mind demanded.

"Well, I still want to talk to you about J.D.," he said. "And it's been a long day. For both of us."

Of course. That explained it, Colleen told herself firmly. He wanted to talk about his father and all she'd managed to do was talk his ear off about *her* problems.

"Okay," she said after a long moment. "That would be nice."

"Great." He stood up and looked down at her. "I'll pick you up at seven."

"I'll give you my address."

"I know where you live," he told her. "I'll see you tonight."

He knew where she lived. What was she supposed to make of that?

"Can I carry your suitcase down to the car?"

"What? Oh. No, thank you." She glanced around the room. "I've still got a few things to pack up."

"All right then, I'll leave you to it," he said, heading for the doorway. When he got there, he paused, turned around and speared her with an unfathomable look. "See you tonight."

When he left, Colleen stared after him for a long minute. Her heartbeat was racing and her knees felt a little wobbly. Her reaction to Sage was so staggering, she wasn't really sure how to deal with it. However, as the sound of his footsteps faded away, Colleen told herself that she couldn't really be blamed for her response to his presence. He was like a force of nature. Sage Lassiter was a gorgeous steamroller, flattening everything in his path.

And Colleen realized that now, for whatever reason, *she* was in his path.

Four

"So how's the rest of dealing with the will going, Walter?" Sage drove straight from Big Blue to the lawyer's office. He wanted a chance to talk to J.D.'s lawyer without the explosive release of emotion that had happened when the family was gathered together. Not that he'd been able to dismiss the anger churning inside him. The plan had been to arrive, calm and cool, and outstare the older man. That didn't happen though, because he was far from feeling cool and detached.

Tension played in every one of his muscles and tugged at the last threads of his patience. Being with Colleen had ramped his body up to the point where he'd practically had to limp his way out of the ranch house. Just sitting beside her on the bed in her room had tested his self-control, because what he'd really wanted to do was lay her back on the mattress and explore those amazing curves she kept so carefully hidden.

Instead, he'd talked to her. And talking to Colleen hadn't solved a damn thing—it had only muddied waters that were already so damn thick it might as well have been concrete. He couldn't make her out. Was she the innocent she seemed to be? Or was she working him as she had worked J.D.? He had to find out…but that was for later. Right now, he had a couple of questions for his late father's lawyer.

"It's coming along but I'm not discussing it with you, Sage, and you damn well know it." Walter Drake steepled his fingers, leaned back in his leather chair and looked at Sage with the barely hidden impatience he would have shown a five-year-old. "J.D.'s will is a private matter. I've already read publicly the parts that affect the family. As for the rest…"

Sage jumped out of his chair and stalked to the far window. Yeah, he was too on edge to be facing down a lawyer. He should have known better than to come here today, but damn it, there were just too many questions about the will.

Looking down on the street below, he focused for a second on the traffic, the pedestrians wandering along the sidewalks and even the mountains jutting into the sky in the distance. He looked anywhere but into the smug features of J.D.'s lawyer.

Going in, Sage had guessed that Walter wouldn't talk. Hell, he wouldn't have even if he *could.* The man liked holding all the power here. Liked having information that no one else did. And getting anything out of him would probably require dynamite—or someone with far more patience than Sage possessed. Fine, then. He'd back off the topic of the rest of the will for the moment and try a different tack. Half turning, he faced the man watching him through hooded eyes.

"All right," Sage said, "never mind."

Walter nodded magnanimously.

"But there's still the matter of J.D. leaving control of Lassiter Media to Evan instead of Angelica."

Walter frowned at him, sat up and braced both elbows on his desktop. "J.D. had reasons for everything he ever did, Sage. You know that."

J.D. had sure thought so. But Sage had given up trying to figure out the old man years ago. The whole time he was growing up, the two of them hadn't even been able to be in the same room together without snarling and growling like a couple of alpha dogs fighting for territory.

But Angelica was different. Right from the start, she had been J.D.'s shining star. So how he could have cut her out of her rightful inheritance was beyond Sage. "Yeah, but what reason could he have for cheating his daughter out of what should have been hers?"

"I can't tell you that."

"Can't?" Sage demanded, walking back to stand opposite the man's desk. "Or won't?"

"Won't." Walter stood up, since staying in his chair required him to look up at Sage, and he clearly didn't enjoy that. "J.D.'s my client, Sage, dead or alive. Not you. Not the Lassiter family."

"And you'll protect him from his damn *family* even after his death?"

"If I have to," Walter said softly.

Frustration clawed at him. "None of this makes sense. You know as well as I do that J.D. had been grooming Angie for years, getting her ready to run Lassiter Media."

"True…"

"So does it seem rational to you that he would leave the company to Angie's fiancé?" There went his grasp on the last slippery thread of temper.

The lawyer only stared at him for a long minute or two. "If you're trying to insinuate that J.D. wasn't competent to make this will, you're wrong. And that allegation would never stand in a court."

"I'm not talking about court." *Yet.* "I'm talking about your knowledge of J.D."

"As I've already said, J.D. had reasons for everything he did, and this is no different."

Sage had no idea why J.D. would have done this. It made no sense at all.

The lawyer's deliberate refusal to give anything away just increased the sense of outrage snarling inside him.

"This isn't getting either of us anywhere, Sage. So if you'll excuse me, I've got business to take care of and—"

"I'm not done with this, Walter," Sage promised. "We all want answers."

For the first time, a flicker of something that might have been sympathy shone in the other man's eyes. "And I wish I could give them to you," he said. "But it's out of my hands."

Frustrated, Sage conceded defeat. At least for now. "Fine. I'll go. But once the family gets over the shock of all of this, I won't be the only one showing up here demanding answers. I hope you're ready for that."

At any other time, Sage might have laughed at the beleaguered expression on the man's face. But right now he just wasn't in the mood to be amused.

Once out in the parking lot, Sage hunched deeper into his black coat as a cold mountain wind pushed at him. Even nature was giving him a hard time today. He crossed to his black Porsche and climbed in. During the winter, this car spent most of its time locked away in a temperature-controlled garage on his ranch. Right now, he was glad he had the sports car. He had a driving need to push the car to its limits, wanting the speed, needing the rush of the moment.

He peeled out of the lot, drove through Cheyenne, and once he was free of the city, cut the powerful engine loose. He backtracked, headed to the Big Blue ranch. By now, Colleen would be gone, but Marlene and Angie would be there. And he had to see his sister. Find out for himself if she was okay. But how could she be? She'd been betrayed by someone she trusted. And Sage knew just how that felt.

The growl of the engine seemed to underscore the rage pumping just below the surface of his mind. Speeding along the road to the ranch forced him to focus, to concentrate on his driving, which gave him a respite from everything else tearing through his brain. He steered the car through the wide ranch gates, kicked up gravel along the winding drive and then parked outside the front doors.

From the stable area came the shouts of men hard at work. He caught a glimpse of a horse in a paddock, running through the dirt, and realized that J.D. being gone hadn't stopped *life* from going on. This ranch would go on, too. The old man had seen to that. But what the hell had he been thinking about the rest of it?

Sage climbed out of the car and paused long enough to take a quick look around the familiar landscape. Much like Sage's own ranch, there were plenty of outbuildings, barns, cabins for the wranglers who lived and worked on the ranch, guest cabins, and even a saltwater pool surrounded by grass, not cement, so that it looked like a natural pond. His gaze fixed on the ancient oak that shaded the pond and a reluctant smile curved his mouth. He, Dylan and Angelica had spent hours out here when they were kids, swinging from a rope attached to one of the oaks' heavy limbs to drop into the cold, clear water.

So much of his life had been spent here on this ranch, and in spite of his estrangement from J.D., there were a lot of *good* memories here, too. He shifted his gaze to the house. Built from hand-cut logs, iron and glass, it was two stories high and boasted wraparound porches with hand-hewn wood railings on both levels. Those porches provided Adirondack chairs with colorful cushions and views of the mountains from almost everywhere.

Sage took a breath. He'd left here only a couple hours ago, but it felt like longer. After mentally dueling with a crafty lawyer, he wanted nothing more than a drink and some quiet. The minute he entered the ranch house, though, he knew the quiet was something that would elude him.

"Why would he do this to me?" Angelica demanded, her voice carrying through the cavernous house.

Three or four people answered her at once and Sage followed the voices to the great room. The heart of the house, the main room was enormous, with honey-toned wood floors, log walls and what seemed like acres of glass windows affording views of the ranch and the wide blue sky that had given the ranch its name above. He'd heard the story often enough to know it by heart.

J.D. and his wife, Ellie, had bought this ranch, then

only two hundred acres, and Ellie had so loved the expanse of deep blue sky that J.D. had decreed the ranch would be named Big Blue, after the sky overhead. Here they'd begun the Lassiter dynasty. Over the years J.D. had added to the property, expanding the ranch into the state's largest cattle herd and building the land holdings up to more than thirty thousand acres. They'd put their stamp on Wyoming and in Cheyenne, the Lassiter name was damn near legend.

Maybe that was part of what Sage had rebelled against all these years. The Lassiter name and what it had meant to J.D. What it had been like to not be born a Lassiter, but *made* into one. With that thought simmering in his brain, he took another step into the chaos.

"Thank heaven," Marlene muttered. "Sage, help me convince your sister that her father wasn't angry at her about anything."

He glanced quickly around the familiar room. The massive stone fireplace, the wide French doors that led to a flagstone patio, the oversize leather couches and chairs dotting the shining wood floor. And the family members scattered across the room, all looking at him.

"What other reason could there be?" Angie asked, throwing both hands high only to let them fall to her sides again. Flipping her dark hair back out of her face, she looked at her oldest brother and said, "I thought he was proud of me. I thought he *believed* in me."

"He did, Angie," Chance put in and she turned on her cousin.

"This is an odd way to show it, don't you think?"

Chance sighed and scrubbed one hand over his face impatiently. Sage could sympathize. The poor guy had probably been trying to cheer Angie up for hours with no success.

"Angie." Evan McCain spoke up then and all eyes turned to him. "You're overreacting."

"Am I?" Shaking her head, Angie looked at the man she had been poised to marry only two weeks ago and it was as if she'd never seen him before. The wedding had been postponed after J.D.'s death, but the two of them had remained close. Until today. Until Evan had been given the company Angie loved. "He gave the company—*my* company—to you, Evan." She slapped one hand to her heart. "I was his daughter and he left it to *you*."

Evan shoved one hand through his hair and looked to Sage for help. But hell, Sage didn't know what he could do. He didn't believe that Evan had tried to undermine Angie. But who the hell knew anymore? Mysterious benefactors. Nurses who inherited three million dollars. A daughter who got cheated out of what should have been hers. None of this made a damn bit of sense.

Still, if they went to war with each other over it, that wouldn't solve a thing either—it would just splinter them when they needed each other most.

"Angie, taking it out on Evan isn't going to help," Sage finally said and he caught a brief look of relief on Evan's face. "We just have to try to figure out what was in J.D.'s mind and then do what we can to change things."

"Can we change anything?" Marlene looked worried, her gaze darting from Angelica to Evan and back again. "The will is done. And even though J.D. was sick, he was mentally competent right up until his last day."

"I know." Sage walked to the woman who had been a mother in all but name to him since he was a kid and wrapped one arm around her shoulders. The scent of her perfume drifted up to him and colored his mind with memories. Marlene had been the one stabilizing influence in his life. Through all of his rebellion with J.D., his aunt was there, talking him down, trying to build a bridge between Sage and his adoptive father. That bridge had never really materialized, but it hadn't been for lack of trying on her part.

Sage dropped a kiss on the top of her head, then looked across the room to Dylan, sprawled in one of the oversize leather chairs.

"You don't have anything to say?"

"I've said plenty," his brother countered, then shifted a glare to their sister. "I was shouted down."

"I didn't shout," Angie argued.

"Like a fishwife," Dylan told her, then glanced at Evan. "If you still want to marry her, you're either brave or brain-dead."

"You're not helping," Sage said.

"Yeah, I heard that from our darling sister an hour ago," Dylan told him tiredly.

"You don't understand how this feels, Dylan," Angelica said, giving him a look that should have set fire to his hair. "Dad didn't take away the business you love, did he?"

"No, he didn't," he admitted.

"Angie," Evan said, stepping toward his fiancée and laying both hands on her shoulders. "I love you. We're getting *married.* Nothing's changed."

She slipped out from under his grip and shook her head. "Everything's changed, Evan. Don't you see that?"

"I don't want to run your company, Angie. You'll

still be doing the day-to-day," he argued. "You're still in charge."

"I don't have the title. I don't have the power. The only reason I would still be in charge is because you *allow* it." She shook her head and bit down hard on her bottom lip before saying, "It's not the same, Evan."

"We'll figure this out," he countered, but Angelica didn't look convinced.

Sage wondered suddenly if maybe J.D. hadn't done all this just so he could hang around as a damn ghost and watch his family jump through the hoops he'd left behind.

"I think we've all had enough for one day," Marlene announced, interrupting what looked as though it could turn into a battle. She walked over to give Angelica a hug, then smoothed a stray lock of her dark brown hair back with gentle fingers. Giving the younger woman a smile, she spoke to the room at large.

"Why don't we all go into the kitchen? We'll have some coffee. Something to eat. It's been a hard day but I think we all have to remember—" she paused, letting her gaze slide around the room "—that we're *family.* We're the *Lassiters.* And we will come through this. Together."

"There's no reason to be so nervous." Jenna Cooper took a sip of her white wine and smiled as Colleen changed clothes for the third time in a half hour.

"I'm not nervous," she replied, "I'm just hyperalert."

Jenna chuckled and curled up into a corner of her chair. Colleen met her friend's amused gaze in the mirror and released a sigh. "Fine. Maybe I'm a little nervous, but there's no reason to be. This is not a date. It's just dinner with a family member of a patient I've lost."

"Uh-huh."

"You might sound a little more convincing when you're placating me."

"I'll work on it," her friend said, still laughing.

Jenna Cooper lived next door, with her husband and adorable three-year-old twin boys, Carter and Cade. At five foot two, Jenna looked like a pixie with very short black hair that curled around her elfin features. Her green eyes were always shining and she and Colleen had been good friends since the second week Colleen had lived in the condo complex two years before.

Knowing Colleen was a nurse, Jenna had come to her door in a panic late one night because one of the boys had had a fever seizure. Colleen had recognized it for what it was immediately and helped them lower Carter's temperature, then she had stayed at the house with a sleeping Cade while Jenna and her husband took Carter to the E.R. to be checked out, just to be on the safe side.

Jenna took a sip of her wine and murmured, "I still can't get over Mr. Lassiter leaving you so much money."

Colleen's stomach churned uneasily and she slapped one hand to her abdomen in a futile attempt to stop it. "Neither can I."

She'd had several hours to think about it, yet it still didn't seem real. Though everything Sage had said to her earlier kept replaying in her mind. The thought of gossip gave her cold chills, but…

"So, have you told your mother yet?"

"About the money?" She shook her head and then frowned at her reflection. Tugging at the scooped bodice, she tried to pull it a little higher, but no matter what she did, you could see cleavage. A *lot* of cleavage. "I never really noticed just how big my boobs are."

"That's because you've usually got them covered up under a layer of cotton and wool." Jenna stood up, smacked Colleen's hand away from the fabric and smiled. "You look gorgeous. Stop fussing. God, that's an amazing dress."

"It is." And ordinarily, she never would have bought anything like it. But Angelica had insisted on taking Colleen shopping for the perfect dress to wear to the re-hearsal dinner. Sage's sister had picked this dress out for Colleen and she'd worn it the night Sage had first noticed her. The night...her eyes widened suddenly. "Oh, God. I can't wear this dress tonight. I was wearing it the night Sage's father collapsed and *died.* What was I thinking?"

She turned to head for her bedroom and the pitiful offerings she might find in her closet, but Jenna stopped her with one hand on her arm. "You can't retire the dress, Colleen. For one thing, it didn't kill Mr. Lassiter, and it's just too amazing to be tossed into the dark abyss that is your closet."

"Thank you."

"And for another thing, trust me when I say that when Sage gets a look at you in this dress—" Jenna took a step back, swept her gaze up and down Colleen and whistled "—it won't be funerals that'll spring to mind."

A tiny thrill dazzled Colleen before she remembered that Jenna was her *friend.* Of course she was going to compliment her. *But,* she told herself firmly, *let's be re-alistic.* Sage Lassiter was *not* interested in her. Going to dinner with him meant absolutely nothing.

"This is crazy," she said aloud. "I'm acting like this is a date and it's not." Colleen wrung her hands together until she realized what she was doing, then she stopped that pitiful action. "Honestly. Slacks and a sweater. That's what I should wear."

"If you change one more time, I'm going to tie you to a chair," Jenna warned. "You look great, you've got a date—"

"Not a date—"

"—you're going to dinner with the most gorgeous man in Wyoming, possibly the United States—"

"I wonder what Tom would say if he heard that."

Jenna grinned. "He's not worried. My Tom's not gorgeous, but he has other…compensations."

"You're impossible." Colleen could admit silently that she felt more than a little envy of her friend's relationship with her very cute husband.

"Tom thinks so…" She grinned again and wiggled her eyebrows for emphasis.

If Colleen had half the confidence that Jenna had, she wouldn't be the slightest bit nervous about her nondate. As it was though…the bats in her stomach—too big for butterflies—were flying in tighter and tighter circles. It was as if they were winding an invisible spring inside her and Colleen was terrified that it was going to snap at just the wrong moment.

Maybe the red dress would help. It was beautiful and wearing it, she couldn't help but feel more confident. Besides, she told herself, Sage might not even remember that she was wearing this dress at the rehearsal dinner.

"Have some wine." Jenna offered her own glass and Colleen snatched at it, taking a big gulp, hoping to drown the bats. Apparently though, they knew how to swim.

"This is a mistake," she muttered and handed the glass back to her friend.

"No, it's not. You're a terrific person, Colleen. It's about time you let some man figure that out for himself."

"It's not a—"

"Yes, yes." Jenna walked back to the love seat, dropped onto the slipcovered cushions and stared up at her. "Now, tell me how my best friend becomes a millionaire and gets a date with *the* Sage Lassiter."

"Weren't you listening? It's *not* a date."

"Whatever." She patted the cushion beside her. "So how're you doing, really, with this crazy, world-shifting, life-altering day?"

Good question. "Actually, I think I'm feeling better about the money."

"Yay!"

Smiling, Colleen thought about sitting down, but she didn't want to wrinkle her dress. How did the beautiful people do this all the time? "Really, I've had all day to think about it, and you know, Sage was right. Even if I give up the money to charity, people will still talk. I'll just be poor while they're talking about me."

"He's obviously brilliant as well as gorgeous. I like him already."

Colleen did, too. Which was worrying on a whole different level. Still, first things first. Now that she'd decided to accept J.D.'s amazing gift, her life was going to change. Big-time. Laughing to herself, she said, "You know this means I can quit my job."

Jenna lifted her glass. "Excellent. Soon-to-be nurse practitioner Colleen Falkner."

Colleen put one hand to her abdomen to ease those bats that were still flying in formation in the pit of her stomach. But it was a futile gesture. Her body had been through so many ups and downs today, there was no

calming it. Oddly enough, it wasn't even the money or
the knowledge that she could make her dreams come
true that was really affecting her. Nope, that was all Sage
Lassiter. His eyes. His mouth. The deep rumble of his
voice, the impossibly broad shoulders.

Oh, God.

She shouldn't be going to dinner with him. Colleen
turned and glanced into the mirror again and what she
saw didn't make her feel any better. Her eyes were too
wide, her boobs were too big, her hair was a mass of
waves on her shoulders because no matter what she'd
tried, she hadn't been able to clip it up and keep it from
looking like a rat's nest.

Why was she putting herself through this? What if
she couldn't talk? What if staring at him across a table
turned her into a mute? Or worse, her mind taunted,
what if she babbled incoherently?

"Stop."

"What?" Colleen came up out of her nerve-racking
thoughts like a drowning woman breaching the surface
of a lake. She was practically gasping for air.

Shaking her head, Jenna said, "You're making yourself nuts. It's just dinner, Colleen. You eat dinner every
day. You can do this."

Could she? She didn't think so. Heck, her last date
had been…oh, God, she couldn't even *remember* when
she'd dated last. All she could recall was that the guy in
question had bored her to tears and then tried to grope
her on her front porch. Good times. "I'm being crazy,
aren't I?"

"Just a little."

"Right." Sage certainly wouldn't be boring, she told
herself. And if he tried to grope her, she might just let

him. Oh, boy. *Get a grip,* she told herself silently. She was making too much of this. Sage wanted to talk about his late father. All she had to do was keep remembering that and she'd be fine. By talking to him, spending time with him, she could help him get the closure he no doubt needed.

This wasn't about *her* and her fantasies. This was about a man, who in spite of his wealth and remarkable good looks, had lost a link to his past. With that thought firmly in mind, she let her sympathy for his loss rise up to drown her silly hormonal meltdown.

"You're right," she said, and reached out to take another sip of Jenna's wine. Colleen hadn't poured herself any because she hadn't wanted to risk alcohol on a nearly empty stomach. But the crisp, sharp taste of the Sauvignon Blanc felt like bliss sliding down her too-tight throat. Then the cold, wheat-colored liquid hit her stomach and immediately soothed those pesky bats.

She took a breath, handed the glass back and checked her reflection one last time. "It's just a meal with a grieving man."

"Yep. Just dinner with the gorgeous, incredibly sexy, unattainable black sheep billionaire," Jenna said with a grin. "No pressure."

Oh, God.

Five

The condo was small, even for a condo.

Sage gave it a quick once-over as he approached the front door. It was tidy, with its cream-colored paint and postage stamp–sized front garden, where spring bulbs were pushing up through the earth. There was a wreath of silk flowers hanging on her front door and when he pushed the doorbell, he wasn't even surprised to hear a series of melodic chimes sounding out from somewhere inside.

What *did* surprise him was Colleen.

She opened the door and every scrap of air escaped from his lungs. She was wearing that red dress again. The one she'd worn the night of the rehearsal dinner. The night he'd really *seen* her for the first time. That damn dress was designed to bring a man to his knees. It molded her figure, defined her luscious breasts and skimmed across rounded hips that made a man think of long, dark nights and hot, steamy sex. Her dark blond hair tumbled over her shoulders and looked like raw honey. He caught the wink of gold earrings when she tossed her hair back and then his gaze dropped lower— to the expanse of smooth, pale flesh that ended in a spectacular display of the tops of her breasts. It was all he could do to lift his gaze to meet her eyes.

"You look beautiful," he said before he could think better of it. Hell, he was always in control of any given situation, and at the moment, he felt like a teenager on his first date. Hard body and vacant mind.

She beamed at him as if he'd handed her flowers, and immediately he told himself he should have done just that. If he was trying to sway her into spilling her secrets, then he should use all the weapons he could bring to bear.

"Thank you," she said, her voice just a little breathless. "Let me get my coat."

She reached into a hall closet, pulled out a heavy black coat and slipped into it, covering herself up so thoroughly, Sage's brain was able to kick back into gear.

She stepped onto the porch, locked her front door, then joined him with another smile. "Shall we go?"

And he knew at that moment, when her blue eyes were staring into his, that this night was not going to go according to plan.

At the restaurant, Sage was grateful for the clink of fine crystal and the murmured conversations that reminded him they were in a public place. Otherwise he might have been in trouble. She was damned distracting, sitting across from him.

"This is lovely," she said, turning her head to look

around the interior of Moscone's Italian restaurant. It was filled with small round tables, covered in white linen and each boasting a single candle in the center. A sleek black-and-chrome bar stood along one wall and Italian arias played softly over the loudspeaker. The floors were tile, the waiters were all in white aprons and the scents filling the air were amazing. "I've never been here before."

"Food's good," Sage mused. "But they're going to have some serious competition when the Lassiter Grill opens up." Damn. He could hardly get words past the knot of need in his throat. Sage took a sip of the wine the waiter had poured just moments before.

"It was really nice of you to bring me here," she said, "but it wasn't necessary. We could have talked at my house."

But then she wouldn't have worn *the dress*. Sage shifted uncomfortably on the black leather bench seat. He hadn't expected to spend the night in agony, but apparently he was going to. And just by looking at her, he knew she had absolutely no idea what she was doing to him. He had to take back control of this situation or he was going to achieve nothing.

"What can you tell me?" he asked, blurting the question out to divert himself from the thoughts plaguing him.

"Anything you want to know."

Like if you talked an old man into leaving you money? Did you steer him away from giving Angelica the company she loves? Did you wear that damn dress on purpose, knowing what it would do to me?

Couldn't start with those questions, though…could

he? His brain scrambled, coming up with a different way to begin.

"First tell me about you. How long have you been a nurse?" Good. Get her talking. Then later, once she'd relaxed her guard, he'd be able to slide the more important questions in.

She took a sip of wine and he watched, hypnotized by the movement in her throat as she swallowed. Not good.

"Eleven years," she said, setting the goblet back onto the table and sliding her fingertips up and down the long, elegant stem.

Sage's gaze fixed on to that motion, and his brain fogged over even as his body went rock hard. He had to force himself to pay attention when she continued to speak quietly.

"When my father got sick, it was such a blessing to be able to help my mom take care of him." Old pain etched itself into her eyes briefly. "After he died, I realized that I was more interested in taking care of people one-on-one than in a hospital setting. I decided to become a private nurse. So I could make a real difference in the lives of families who were going through what we went through."

Was she really as selfless and kind as she appeared? He wanted to spot deception, gamesmanship in her eyes, but those soft blue depths remained as clear and guileless as ever. Was she really that good an actress, he wondered. Or was she really an innocent?

No, he mentally assured himself. There were no innocents anymore. And a woman this staggeringly beautiful had no doubt learned before she was five just how to work a man.

Pleased that he'd managed to wrest control of his

own urges, he asked, "How long ago did you lose your father?"

"Six years," she said softly and her features once again twisted with sorrow.

"Then," she added, "Mom and I both decided we needed a change, a chance to get away from the memories, so we left California and came here."

"Why Cheyenne?"

She laughed a little and her blue eyes sparkled with it. Instantly, his control drowned in a sea of pulsing desire that grabbed hold of him and wouldn't let go.

"You won't believe it."

"Try me."

"Okay." She leaned in a little closer, as if telling a funny story. Unfortunately, this increased his view of the delectable cleavage that dress displayed.

"We laid a map of the U.S. out on the dining room table and Mom closed her eyes and poked her finger down. She hit Cheyenne and here we are."

Surprise and a bit of admiration rose up inside him, however reluctantly. "Just like that. You packed up and moved to somewhere you'd never been before."

"It was an adventure," she told him with a smile. "And we both needed one. Watching someone you love die by inches is horrible. At least you were spared that. I know it's not much comfort though."

He didn't speak because, frankly, what the hell could he say? She'd obviously had a much better relationship with her father than he'd had with his.

"Although," she added, "the snow was hard to get used to. We're California girls through and through, so we needed a whole new wardrobe when we got here."

"I can imagine." His mind brought up the image of

her seeing her first snowfall, and he almost wished he'd been there to witness it.

"When your winter coat is a sweatshirt and you can wear flip-flops year-round…" Another bright smile. "Let's just say it was even more of an adventure than we'd thought it would be."

"But you enjoy it?"

"I love it," she said simply. "I'd never had a change of season before. I love the fall. And the snow is so beautiful. Then the spring when everything comes alive again. Mostly though, I love the mountains."

"Me, too." Funny, he hadn't thought they'd find common ground, but here it was. Unless, his mind chided, she was saying what she thought he wanted to hear. After all, if J.D. had talked about him as she said, then she knew Sage owned a ranch in the high country, and why else would he do that if he didn't love the mountains?

"I know… J.D. told me about your ranch."

Ha! Proof then. But he played along. "If I can help it, I rarely come down off the mountain into the city."

"I know that, too," she said, her hand stilling on the wineglass. "J.D. talked about you a lot. How you preferred your ranch to anywhere else in the world. He missed seeing you, but said that you almost never left the ranch."

A flare of something hot slashed through him. Guilt? He didn't *do* guilt. "J.D. didn't have much room to talk. You could hardly blast him off the Big Blue with a stick of dynamite."

"True," she said, agreeing with him. "He told me. Truth is, he used to worry that you were too much like him. Too ready to cut yourself off from everything."

"I'm not cut off." Hadn't Dylan said the same thing

to him just hours ago? Why did everyone assume that because a man was happy where he was that he was missing out on other things?

"Aren't you?" It was softly asked, but no less invasive.

He stiffened and the desire pumping through him edged back just a little. Sage hadn't brought her there to talk about *him*.

"No," he assured her, and even he heard the coolness in his tone. "Just because I didn't visit J.D. doesn't mean I'm a damn hermit."

Hermits had a hell of a lot more peace and quiet than he ever got. It wasn't that Sage didn't love his family, he did. He only preferred the solitude of his ranch because nothing good ever came of mixing with people—

He cut that thought off and buried it amid the rubble of his memories.

"He missed you."

Three words that hurt more than he would have thought possible. Sage and J.D. had been at odds for so many years, it was hard to remember a time when things were different. He didn't want to feel another sting of guilt, but how the hell could he avoid it? J.D. had been old and sick and still Sage hadn't been able to get past their differences. Would that haunt him for the rest of his life? Would he have yet another regret to add to the multitude he already carried?

Shaking his head, he told her, "Our arguments were legendary. J.D. and I mixed about as well as oil and water. There's just no way he missed me, so you don't have to worry about telling pretty lies and trying to make me feel better. I know the truth."

About that, anyway.

"It's not a lie," she said, pausing for another sip of her wine.

What was it about the woman's throat and the slim elegance of it that fascinated him?

"He did miss you." She smiled at him again and the warmth in her eyes washed over him. "He told me about your arguments. And really, I think he missed them. He had no one to butt heads with, and that must have been frustrating for a man as strong and powerful as he once was."

Frowning now, Sage saw that she might just have a point. Even though his relationship with J.D. had never been a close one, he knew that his adoptive father had gone through life like a charging bull. Putting his head down and rushing at problems, determined to knock them out of his way through sheer force of will.

J.D. Lassiter had been the kind of man who let nothing stand between him and his goals. He'd bent the world to his whim and pushed those around him into line—or in Sage's case, had *tried* to. For him to be reduced to a sick bed because his heart had turned on him must have been wildly frustrating. Surprisingly, Sage felt a twinge of sympathy for the old man rattle around inside him before he could stop it.

"He told me that he and his wife adopted you and Dylan when you were boys."

Seemed J.D. had talked her damn ears off. Which gave him hope that somewhere in there, he might have confessed the reasons behind his will.

"They did," he said and reluctantly was tossed into the past.

He had been six and Dylan four when they went to live on Big Blue. Their parents had just been killed in a traffic accident and they'd clung to each other in an unfamiliar world. Then J.D. and Ellie had swooped in and suddenly, everything was different. Their lives. Their home. Their parents. All new. All so damned hard to accept. At least for Sage. Dylan, maybe because he was younger, had accepted the change in their lives with much more ease.

Sage had refused to let go of his memories…of the life he'd been forced to surrender. He'd bucked against the rules, had fought with his new parents and in general been a pain in the ass, now that he thought about it. He'd grumbled about everything, comparing their new life to the old and the new always came up short.

Ellie had tried relentlessly, through patience and love, to get through to Sage and eventually she'd succeeded. But J.D. hadn't had the patience to carefully win Sage over. Instead, he'd simply demanded respect and affection and Sage had refused to give either.

The two of them had fought over everything, he remembered now. From doing chores as a kid to driving as a teenager. Sage had instinctively gone in the opposite direction of anything J.D. recommended. There'd been plenty of battles between them, with Ellie stepping in as peacemaker—until she died after giving birth to Angelica.

And the love they shared for Sage's sister was the one thing he and J.D. had ever agreed on. She had been the glue in their shattered family. Without Ellie there, they would have all floundered, but caring for Angelica kept them all afloat. Then Marlene had moved in and because she hadn't expected their love, she'd won their hearts.

Shaking his head now, Sage reached for his wine and gulped it down as if it were water. The waiter appeared, delivering their meals, and for a moment or two, there was silence. Then they were alone again and Colleen finally spoke.

"I'm sorry. I didn't mean to bring back unpleasant memories."

"You didn't," he lied, smoothing his voice out as easily as he mentally paved over memory lane.

"Okay." She took a small bite of her ravioli, then chewed and swallowed. "Well, I've been talking forever. Why don't you tell me about your ranch?"

Sage stared at her for a long minute as he tried to figure out what she was up to. But damned if he could see signs of manipulation on her features.

So he started talking, grateful to be in comfortable territory. He watched her face as she listened to him, and enjoyed the shift and play of emotions she made no attempt to hide. But as he told her about his place, Sage realized something. He wasn't going to be getting the information he needed tonight. She was either really skillful at turning the conversation away from her—or she was as sweet and innocent as she appeared to be. But either way, it was going to take longer than he'd thought to find out exactly what she knew.

Oddly enough, that thought didn't bother him at all.

"You can't be serious." Laura Falkner dropped into her favorite chair and stared up at her daughter as if she'd just sprouted another head. "Three million dollars?"

Colleen drew a deep breath and realized that over the past few days, she had actually gotten *used* to the idea of having three million dollars. Okay, it was still a little weird to know that she wasn't going to have to worry about paying her cable bill—or anything else. But she'd finally come to grips with the idea that J.D. had meant for her to have this. That he'd wanted to help her reach her dreams, and she only wished that she could look him in the eye and say *thank you*.

Now, seeing her mother's reaction to her news made Colleen excited all over again. She was so glad she'd waited a few days to tell her mom. Colleen had wanted to get everything in order, have her plan set in stone so her mom couldn't argue with her over any of it. It hadn't been easy to wait. The past three days had been a whirlwind of activity. She'd hardly had a chance to really sit down and appreciate just how much her life had changed.

And thanks to J.D.'s generosity, her mother's life was about to change, too.

Looking around the apartment she and her mom had shared when they first moved to Cheyenne, Colleen smiled. There were good memories here, but soon her mother would be making new memories. Enjoying the dreams she'd always tucked aside. And that pleased her, even though she knew she would miss her mom being so close by.

"I'm completely serious," Colleen replied, sitting in the chair opposite her mother. She reached out and took her mom's hands in hers. "It's all true. I'm going to get my nurse practitioner's license and buy myself a cabin in the mountains as soon as possible."

"Honey, that's wonderful." Laura pulled her hands free of her daughter's grasp, then cupped Colleen's face between her palms. "It's been your dream for so long, having a rural practice." Leaning back in her chair, she smiled even more broadly. "I'm delighted for you. Of course I was so sad to hear that Mr. Lassiter had died, but it was so good of him to remember you."

"It really was." She could see that now and accept J.D.'s bequest for the gift it was. She didn't care anymore if people talked. As Sage had pointed out, either way, she couldn't stop them, so why shouldn't she be grateful to J.D. and enjoy what he'd tried to give her?

Sage.

Just the thought of his name sent ripples of anticipation racing through her. It had been three days since their dinner together, and the one-time-only night to talk about J.D. had turned into something more. Sage had taken her to a movie two nights ago, and last night to a country-western club for dancing. She still didn't understand why he wanted to spend so much time with her, but she was enjoying herself more than she would have thought possible.

Dragging herself away from thoughts of Sage, Colleen focused on what she'd come to tell her mother. "There's more, Mom."

"More?" Laura just blinked at her. "You have financial security. You're about to make your dream job a reality. What's left?"

"Your dreams."

"What?" Her mother had the wary look in her eyes that she used to get when Colleen was a child and up to something.

"You know how you're always talking about moving to Florida to live with Aunt Donna?"

The two sisters were both widows now, and they'd discussed for years how much fun it would be if they could live together. But neither of them had been able to afford the move, so it just hadn't been possible. Until now.

"Yessss…"

"Well, you're going to."

"I'm—" Her mother's mouth snapped shut. "Don't be silly."

"It's not silly." Colleen had it all worked out in her mind. In fact, since the reading of the will three days before, she'd spent a lot of time on the phone, talking to lawyers, bankers, real estate agents and travel agencies. She had wanted every detail clear in her mind before broaching the subject to her mother. It had all been worth it, too, because as she started laying out her plans, Laura was dumbstruck.

"I've found a perfect house for you and Aunt Donna. It's gorgeous and it's in this lovely retirement community outside Orlando."

"You can't do that, you don't have the money yet and—"

Colleen cut her off quickly. "It's amazing how willing banks are to give you a line of credit based on a lawyer's sworn affidavit that a will's bequest is coming."

"You didn't."

"Oh, yes, I did." Walter Drake wasn't the easiest lawyer to talk to, but he had assured Colleen that she would be able to draw on her bequest almost immediately. And he'd gone out of his way to set up the line of credit with a local bank.

Laura pushed out of the chair and walked the few steps to the narrow, galley-style kitchen. Busily, she filled a teakettle with water and set it on the stove, all the while shaking her head and muttering.

"Mom—"

"You shouldn't have done that, Colleen," her mother said, not even looking at her. She turned the fire on under the kettle, then grabbed two mugs from a cupboard and dropped a tea bag into each of them. "I don't want you spending money on me. I want you to have that money to keep you safe."

Colleen's heart turned over. Her mom was the most unselfish person she'd ever known in her life. She always gave and never once had she done anything purely for herself. Well, that was about to change, whether she liked it or not.

Joining her mother in the kitchen, Colleen gave her a hard hug, then said, "I couldn't spend all of that money if I tried and you know it."

"Just the same—"

"Mom." Colleen tried another tack. "Getting a house for you and Donna, so you can live without the snow making your arthritis worse, that makes me feel *great*. And, I only put a down payment on it. I would never buy you a house you haven't even seen."

"I don't like this…"

"You will," Colleen said, hugging her again. "And anyway, if you don't like the house, we'll find something else. I just thought it would be a good idea because this community has people to take care of your yard and watch over your house while you're traveling—"

"Traveling?"

This was so much fun, it was like Christmas morning. Colleen grinned. "Yes. You're going to travel. Just like you always wanted to."

"Honey, enough. You know I can't let you do this. Any of it." Laura finally found her voice and naturally she was using it to try to turn down her daughter's generosity.

"Too late, it's already done." Colleen hurried back into the living room, grabbed her purse and carried it back to the kitchen. She set it onto the small round table, slid one hand inside and came back up with a batch of cruise brochures. Handing them over to her mother, she tapped her index finger on the top one.

"A world cruise?" Laura dropped into one of the kitchen chairs as if she'd suddenly gone boneless.

"Yes." Colleen really did feel like Santa. A tall, busty Santa with big feet. "It doesn't leave for another three months, though, so you and Aunt Donna have plenty of time to get your passports and shopping done, and I thought we could talk about your moving to Florida as soon as you get back. Of course, if you'd rather move right away, I understand, but I don't know that I'm ready to have you leave just yet and…"

She stopped talking when she saw the tears spill from her mother's eyes and run down her cheeks. "Don't cry. You're supposed to be happy! Did I mention that you and Aunt Donna are going to be sharing the presidential suite on your cruise? There are pictures in the brochure. You have a full balcony. And butler service and twenty-four-hour room service and—"

Laura choked out a laugh, then lifted one hand to her mouth, shaking her head in disbelief.

"Mom, are you okay?"

"I don't think so," she murmured, staring down at the brightly colored brochures displaying pictures of England, Scotland, Switzerland and more. "I can't let you do this, honey…"

"Mom." Colleen hugged her mother tightly, then leaned back and looked into watery blue eyes much like her own. "You've given me everything for so long. I want to do this. I *can* do this now and if you fight me on it—"

Laura laughed a little again. "You'll what?"

"I'll hold my breath." She smiled, hoping to coax an answering smile from her mother. Holding her breath had been her threat of choice when she was a little girl and using it now was a deliberate choice.

"You never could stop talking long enough to hold your breath for long," her mother finally said, and Colleen knew she'd won.

"Well, I had very important things to say. Just like now." She plucked one of the brochures from her mother's hands and spread it open, showing the sumptuous cabin her mother and aunt would be sharing on their twelve-week cruise. "Just look at this, Mom. Can you imagine?"

"No," she said, sliding one hand across the high-gloss paper, "I really can't."

"I'm going to want lots of pictures cluttering up my in-box."

"I'll email every day." She frowned. "They do have computers on board, right?"

"Absolutely. Complete with Skype. We can talk face-to-face whenever you have time." As she thought about it, she said, "Maybe we'll get you a computer tablet, too, so you can video chat with me from Stonehenge!"

"Donna's not going to believe this," her mother whispered, unable to tear her gaze away from the pictures of a dream of a lifetime coming true.

Six

A few hours later, Colleen sat across from Sage in a local coffee shop. "You should have seen my mother's face," she said, grinning at the memory.

"She must have been shocked." He could imagine. Hearing her talk about what she'd done for her mother had stunned Sage into silence himself.

Far from the grasping, manipulative woman he'd assumed her to be, she'd arranged for her mother and aunt to have the trip they'd always dreamed instead of spending her money on herself. Admiration flowed through him, along with the desire that had become as familiar to him as breathing over the past few days.

Since that first dinner hadn't brought him any information, Sage had made it his business to spend as much time with Colleen as possible. Though they hadn't been able to speak at the movies, watching her reaction to the drama playing out on the screen had fascinated him. Tears, laughter, a jolt of surprise at the happy ending—she was so easy to read and at the same time, so damn complicated he didn't know what to make of her.

Long ago, he had decided that women weren't to be trusted. That they turned their emotions on and off at whim, the better to acquire whatever they happened to be after at the time. Tears were a woman's best weapon, as he'd discovered early on. But on the surface, at least, Colleen seemed...different.

And that both intrigued and worried him.

"Oh, she really was." Shaking her head, she picked up her burger and took a bite, still smiling. "Mom and Aunt Donna have been planning fantasy trips for years. They go back and forth, deciding what hotels they'll stay in, what countries they'll see. They go online and look up cruise packages, just to torture themselves." She took a breath and sighed happily. "Knowing that they're going to actually get to go and *experience* everything they've always talked about is just...amazing."

"*You're* amazing," he murmured, thinking his voice was so soft it would be lost in the clatter and noise from the rest of the patrons surrounding them.

He should have known she'd hear him.

"Why?"

Sage shrugged, sat back in the booth and draped one arm along the back. "Most people, receiving a windfall like you did? They'd go out and buy themselves fast cars, a house that's too big and too expensive, all kinds of things. But you didn't. You bought your mother's dreams."

She smiled. "What a nice way to put it."

Her eyes were shining and that smile lit her face up

like a damn beacon. Something inside him turned over and he was pretty sure it was his heart. That was unsettling. Sage had spent most of his life carefully building a wall around his heart, keeping out anything that might touch him too deeply. His family was one thing. His brother and sister were a part of him, and he accepted the risk of loving them because there was no way he could live without them.

But to love a woman? To trust love? No. He'd nearly made that mistake years ago, and he'd steered clear of it ever since. He'd had a narrow escape and hadn't come away unscathed even at that. So the women he allowed into his life now were nothing like Colleen. They were temporary distractions…just blips on a radar that was finely tuned for self-protection. Colleen was something different. If she was who he now believed her to be, then he had no business being around her. But for the life of him, he couldn't stay away.

Frowning now, he said, "What about your plans? Your dreams?"

She picked up her iced tea and took a long drink. "Well, I already told you my main goal. I'm going to get my nurse practitioner's license."

"Because?"

"Because what I'd really like to do is have a rural practice," she said, leaning toward him over the table.

He caught himself wishing she was wearing that red dress again so he could get another peek at her luscious breasts. Instead though, she wore an emerald-green sweater over a white T-shirt with a slightly V-shaped neckline. Her jeans were soft and faded and hugged her curves like a lover's hands. And even the casual clothing couldn't dispel the desire that pumped through him just sitting across from her.

For a man who prided himself on his rational thinking and ability to concentrate on the task at hand, it grated that while she talked, all he could think about was laying her down atop the table and burying himself deep inside her.

"There are a lot of people in the high country who live so remotely it's hard to get into town to see a doctor," she was saying and he could read the excitement on her face with every word she spoke. "Or if they can, they can't afford it."

She kept surprising him.

Wanting to devote herself to a rural practice would be a hard, even dangerous way to build a career. Why wasn't she like other women? Why wasn't she making plans for spa trips and exclusive shopping excursions? Hell, she'd bought her mother and aunt an around-the-world cruise. But for herself, she wanted to live and work in the wilderness areas?

That thought settled in his mind and his brain drew up a series of uncomfortable images. Colleen trying to dig her way out of a blizzard. Colleen's little Jeep careening off a mountain road and sailing down into a rock-strewn canyon. Colleen freezing to death in her car because she'd gotten lost.

His stomach twisted into knots and he told himself that it was none of his business if she wanted to risk her life by working somewhere she had no knowledge of. He was only with her to find out what she knew. There was no real relationship between them. She wasn't his to protect.

But damn it, *someone* had to set her straight.

"Driving up into the mountains from Cheyenne is going to make for a hell of a commute. Especially in winter," he pointed out, with a warning note in his tone that he hoped would get past the spirit of adventure he saw so clearly in her eyes.

Colleen flashed him a smile that shone from those cornflower-blue eyes and hit him like a sledgehammer.

"That's part two of my plan," she said, clearly pleased with herself. "I'm not going to be commuting every day. That would be silly and time-consuming. Instead, I'm selling my condo and I'm going to buy a cabin or a small house higher up in the mountains."

Those mental images rose up again, only this time, he saw Colleen in a remote cabin, no help for miles around. An icicle dropped down his spine.

"And live there by yourself?" He didn't like the sound of that. Not that there were a million crazies running around the mountains or anything, but hell, you didn't need a human enemy to worry about. Nature could kill you just for the hell of it. And nature in the wilderness had attitude.

"I'm a big girl," she countered, airily brushing aside his concerns. "I can take care of myself."

"No doubt," he said, though he doubted it very much. "In the city. Where there are police to call if you need help. Neighbors right next door. Grocery stores. Not to mention that you grew up in California. What do you know about digging yourself out of ten-foot snowdrifts or how to stockpile firewood for winter? What do you know about driving on roads that haven't been cleared by the county after a storm?"

She frowned a little, then took a breath and admitted,

"Okay, there's a learning curve. But I can adapt. I'll figure it out as I go. It'll be another adventure."

"Learning as you go can turn it into a *final* adventure."

Sighing, Colleen pushed her lunch plate to one side, apparently losing her appetite as they talked. She took another sip of her iced tea, then set the glass down. "Why are you raining on my parade, Sage? You live up on the mountain and you love it."

"This isn't about shooting down your dreams, Colleen," he said tightly. "This is about being realistic. Thinking things through."

"I have thought it through. I've *been* thinking about this for years." She leaned even closer and Sage was caught in her eyes. "I could make a real difference in people's lives."

"Or end your own," he told her, hating that the shine in her eyes dimmed a little at his words. But better she be disappointed than in danger. "I was raised up there, Colleen. I know how to survive bad weather. More than that, I know not to turn my back on the mountain. I don't take anything for granted."

"You weren't born knowing all of that, though," she said, determination clear in her voice. "You learned. So can I."

Sage tore his gaze from hers and glanced around the coffee shop. He needed a minute to get ahold of himself. To keep from *ordering* her to stay off the damn mountain. Conversations rose and fell from the dozens of customers gathered in the sunlit restaurant. An occasional burst of laughter rang out, and the scent of coffee and hamburgers hung in the air. Coming here to the coffee shop had seemed like a good idea at the time. With the amount of tension he'd been living with the past few days, he'd figured that taking Colleen to a crowded place in the middle of the day was one way to help him keep a tight grip on his control. Naturally, that wasn't working out as he'd planned. Pretty much nothing had since he'd first met Colleen.

Shaking his head grimly, Sage noticed the number of strange faces among the crowd. Tourists were streaming into Cheyenne already, clogging up the streets and making the restaurants even more crowded than usual. Soon, the summer crowds would be arriving. By the end of July, thousands would be here for Cheyenne Frontier Days, reliving the Old West and enjoying the world's largest outdoor rodeo. There would be ten days of parades, carnivals and food fairs. For a second, he thought about the rodeo itself and remembered what it had been like to ride in front of thousands of cheering people.

Of course, it wasn't just the rodeo that drew people to Cheyenne. Summer was filled with tourist attractions from the eight-foot-tall painted fiberglass cowboy boots situated all over the city to the carefully staged, G-rated "gunfights" acted out daily by the Cheyenne Gunslingers. There were tours, art festivals and so many other activities, people came to Cheyenne and poured hundreds of thousands of dollars into the local economy.

As for Sage, he tried to stay on the mountain to avoid all of those people. He spent summers working with the horses and trying to forget that there was a world outside his ranch. Right now, though, summer was still months away and Sage's mind was preoccupied by the thought of Colleen, midwinter, all alone on the mountain. Cold dropped into the pit of his stomach and stayed there.

He shifted his gaze back to hers and barked, "You can't do it."

"Excuse me?" Her face went blank for an instant, and then her cheeks flushed with color and her eyes started firing sparks at him.

"Maybe I put that the wrong way," he allowed, since he hadn't been thinking at all when the words shot from his throat.

"You think?"

Colleen felt a quick spurt of irritation, then squashed it again quickly. Yes, Sage was being a little authoritarian, but he had backed off quickly, too, hadn't he? It was in his nature to take command. She could tell that by the way he stood, so tall and alert, his gaze constantly darting around his surroundings, as if checking for any problem that might arise. He was the kind of man who would always do what he could to keep people safe— whether they appreciated it or not.

And now, he was trying to protect *her*. Which made her feel good enough that she was willing to overlook the fact that he was also trying to keep her from doing what she'd always dreamed of doing. Actually, she could hardly believe she was out with him. Again. And the past few times she'd been with him had absolutely been dates.

Even Jenna agreed that this had moved way beyond him wanting closure after his father's death. There was something else going on here. They rarely talked about J.D. anymore, instead sharing stories about their lives and talking about everyday things. So if it wasn't about his dad, what else could it be? She wasn't sure, but she had decided to simply enjoy this time with Sage for as long as it lasted. Because she knew, at the heart of it, she just wasn't the kind of woman to capture and hold the interest of a man like him.

"I didn't mean that you *can't*," he was saying and Colleen came up out of her thoughts to focus her attention on him. "What I meant was that you can't just decide to live in what could be dangerous terrain while knowing nothing about survival." Colleen couldn't help it—she laughed. He looked so serious. So…growly. A small, tiny part of her thrilled to hear him trying protect her. But the reality was, she took care of herself very well.

"You make it sound as though I'm talking about moving to the middle of nowhere. This isn't the frontier, Sage. I'll be perfectly safe."

"Probably," he agreed, "but the country—especially the *high* country—can be dangerous."

She shook her head, then pushed her hair back from her face and gave him a patient smile. "How dangerous can it be, really?"

"Bears?" he fired back.

Before she could react to that disturbing thought, he continued.

"Mountain lions? Snakes? Blizzards?" He picked up his coffee and took a drink. "You're not in any way prepared for that kind of life, Colleen. You're asking for trouble if you do this."

He was right. She hadn't really considered any of that, and she could admit, at least to herself, that the thought of facing any *one* of those dangers on her own was… intimidating. All right, terrifying. But there had to be a way to make this work. "Fine, I admit you have a point."

He nodded.

"*But* if I knew how to handle myself in those situations, I'd be okay, right?"

"Sure," he said, one corner of his mouth curving up. "*If.* And that's a big *if.*"

"You could teach me."

"What?" He paused, coffee cup halfway to his mouth.

The idea had just leaped into her mind, but now that it was there, she ran with it. J.D. had told her so much about Sage—there was no one she would trust more to show her what she needed to know. "I promise, I'm a quick study. And you said yourself that you grew up in the mountains. No one knows them better than you do, right?"

"I suppose…" He set his still-steaming mug of coffee down onto the table and stared at her. And that penetrating stare was so…disconcerting, it was hard to draw an easy breath. His eyes were just hypnotic. At least to Colleen. Honestly, she was proud of herself just for being able to speak coherently while looking into those deep blue eyes of his. His jaw was tight, his dark brown brows drawn into a scowl, and still she thought he was the most gorgeous man she'd ever seen.

Every time he looked at her, she felt that swirl of batwings in the pit of her stomach—not to mention heat that burned just a bit lower. She'd never been so aware of herself as a woman as she was when she was with Sage Lassiter. He made her feel things she'd never experienced before and *want* things she knew she shouldn't.

Being with him was a kind of pleasurable torture, which had to be an oxymoron or something, but she really couldn't think of another way to put it. She enjoyed his company, but her body was constantly buzzing out of control around him, too. Which left her breathless, on edge and in a constant state of excitement. It was the most alive she'd felt in years.

"What do you think, Sage?" She kept her gaze fixed on his. "Will you show me what I need to know?"

His features froze and she watched a muscle in his jaw twitch spasmodically. His fingers drummed against the tabletop and he shifted in his seat. He was thinking about it, and Colleen anxiously waited to see what he would say.

Finally, her patience was rewarded.

"You want to learn to survive on the mountain."

"Yes." She bit her bottom lip.

"Fine," he said. "I'll teach you."

A wash of relief and something that felt like eager anticipation swept through her. "That's *great,* thank you."

He laughed shortly. "Save your thanks. By the time we're finished, you'll probably be cursing me."

"No, I won't." She shook her head and reached across the table to cover one of his hands with hers. "J.D. always told me how kind you were and I've really seen that for myself in the past few days."

He just stared at her through eyes that had been carefully shuttered. "J.D. was wrong. I'm not kind, Colleen."

His features were hard, his body language cold. He was pulling back from her even while he was within reach. She didn't know why. "If it's not kindness," she asked quietly, "what is it?"

He just looked at her for a long moment and she had the feeling he was trying to decide whether to answer her or not. Then she got her answer.

"You said you don't have a job to go to anymore, right?"

"No, I don't. I turned in my resignation at the agency." And hadn't that felt incredible? She had liked her job well enough, but now that her dream was within her reach, she didn't mind at all saying goodbye to the private agency. "Until I get my practitioner's license, I'm officially unemployed."

"All right then," he said, coming to some internal decision. "We'll start day after tomorrow. You come up to my ranch and stay for a few days. We'll go up the mountain from there."

"Stay? At your ranch?" Heat sizzled through her veins, and even while a delicious tingle settled deep inside her, Colleen felt a tiny niggle of worry.

He was going to teach her to survive in the mountains. But who could teach her how to survive a broken heart when this time with him was over?

Logan Whittaker was handsome, friendly and professional. Late thirties, he was tall, with nearly black hair, warm brown eyes and when he smiled, a disarming pair of dimples appeared in his cheeks. He wore a sports coat over a pair of black jeans and a long-sleeved white shirt, black cowboy boots betraying his Texas heritage.

As a partner at Drake, Alcott and Whittaker, he was able to meet with Colleen the next morning, when Walter Drake was busy elsewhere.

She walked into his office and took a quick, admiring look around. The room was huge, befitting a partner. Neutral colors, with navy blue accents, including a navy blue sofa and matching visitor chairs situated on one side of his massive desk. There was a blue-and-white-tiled fireplace on one wall with an empty mantel over it. No family pictures to clutter up his office.

The windows along the hallway boasted electric shades that were in a halfway-down position. It was all very businesslike but hospitable, much like Logan himself seemed to be.

"I really appreciate you seeing me on such short notice."

"Not a problem," Logan said, stepping forward to take her hand in a firm shake before steering her toward one of the visitor's chairs. "Walter and I are sort of working a tag team on the Lassiter will. We're each dealing with different angles, and sometimes the lines cross."

She had to smile. The slight hint of a Texas accent flavored his speech, but couldn't hide the fact that he seemed agitated and a little harried. "Having some trouble with J.D.'s will?"

He blew out a breath, took a seat in his chair behind the wide desk and then shot her a heart-stopping grin. "Is it that obvious?" A short laugh rumbled from his throat as he shook his head. "Let's just say there are some issues with the estate that I'm not at liberty to discuss and leave it at that."

"Well, that sounds frustrating."

"Oh, it is." He pushed one hand through his hair and said, "But I'll get it done."

The look in his eyes was sheer determination, and Colleen didn't doubt for a minute that he would succeed.

"Now, how can I help you, Ms. Falkner?"

"Colleen, please." She scooted forward to the edge of the leather chair and leaned her forearm on his desk. "Walter helped me set up a line of credit at a local bank, but—"

"What is it?" He gave her his full attention, and Colleen thought at any other time, she might have been mesmerized by his eyes. The man was exceptionally good-looking and when he looked at a woman with his complete concentration, she could only assume that most women melted into a puddle at his feet. As it stood now, though, Logan Whittaker, as handsome and compelling as he was, couldn't hold a candle to Sage Lassiter.

Letting go of that train of thought, she brought herself back to the business at hand. The reason she'd come here.

"I really just wanted to make sure everything is going through without any trouble." Shrugging, she added, "I'm about to sell my condo so I can buy something closer to where I will be working, and—"

He gave her a knowing smile. "And you're worried that something might go wrong with the dispersal of the will."

"Exactly." It was nice that he understood her concerns and didn't make her feel silly for having them.

"You have nothing to worry about," Logan told her. "J.D. set this will up in such a way that it would be almost impossible to contest it."

"Almost?"

He grinned. "Caught that, did you?"

"I did, and it's a little scary to think about. If someone contested the will, all of the bequests might be nullified, right?"

"It's possible, yes," he admitted, then leaned back in his oversize leather swivel chair. "But highly unlikely. J.D. was competent when he made his will. And it was his estate to divide how he saw fit. I know some of the family are upset with what that will said, but there's not much they can do about it. So to answer your question, I don't see any problems looming. Go ahead and sell your place. Buy the one you want."

Colleen released a breath she really hadn't been aware she was holding. Somehow she felt even more reassured than she had when talking to Walter. Maybe it was because the older lawyer tended to speak more in legal terms, and Logan made the process seem less confusing. "Thanks. I feel better."

"Happy to help," Logan said, rising to come around his desk. "I know this must be strange, suddenly coming into so much money. But it's all real, Colleen. You can trust it."

She stood up and offered her hand. This was what she'd needed to hear: the confirmation that her new life was about to begin. For some reason, she'd been half expecting someone to pull the rug out from under her and leave her sprawled, broken and bruised, on the floor. Metaphorically speaking, of course.

Now though, she would reach out and grab hold— with both hands—of the changes headed her way.

Logan walked her to his door and smiled. "Try to relax and enjoy all of this, Colleen. J.D. clearly wanted that for you."

"I think he did," Colleen agreed as she shook Logan's hand one last time. "I really appreciate your time."

"If you have any more worries, feel free to come back."

But she wouldn't be worried now. At least not about the bequest. Instead, she would worry about Sage Lassiter and how important he was becoming to her. When just the thought of his name sent an electrical charge buzzing through her, she knew she had *plenty* to worry about.

Seven

"Wow," Jenna chirped later that day. "According to Google, Sage Lassiter is worth about ten *billion* dollars." She glanced up from the laptop and fanned herself with one hand. "I mean I knew he was rich…but that is *seriously* rich."

The two of them were in Colleen's bedroom at her condo. The room was small but neat, with cream-colored walls, a bright quilt on the bed and dozens of jewel-toned pillows stacked against the headboard. Colleen looked at her friend, sitting cross-legged on her bed. "You're supposed to be checking real estate on the mountain for me."

"I am, on another webpage," Jenna said with a shrug. "But I can multitask. Besides, I had to look him up. You're going to stay at his ranch for a few days and I want to see what my friend's getting into. You know, I bet there are rich serial killers, too."

Laughing, Colleen said, "He's not a serial killer."

"No harm in checking," Jenna told her. "So, according to this website that is all gossip all the time, Sage made his first million by investing in some thingama-jig for computers that his college roommate invented."

"Well, that tells me he believed in his friend, so that's nice."

"And made a boatload off that investment," Jenna continued, scrolling down the page, "which he then invested in several other inventors with great ideas."

"That's a good thing. He helped a lot of people get started and they all became successes." Colleen folded another T-shirt and dropped it into her suitcase. She would drive up to Sage's ranch in the morning and nerves were beginning to settle in. Three days at his house. God, she could hardly sit across from him in a restaurant without her body erupting in dangerous wants and needs. The next few days were going to be agonizing.

Unless, she thought wildly, something happened between them to release all this tension she felt building inside her. But if they did sleep together, then what? From everything she'd learned from J.D., she knew that Sage wasn't interested in a real relationship. And even if he were, he wouldn't want her, she knew that already.

So what would she gain by going to bed with him?

Lovely memories, her brain shrieked. *Orgasms galore,* her body chimed in.

She shivered again.

This had seemed like such a good idea, having Sage show her the mountains and how to avoid danger.

Which was really funny if you thought about it, because Sage himself was dangerous to her. He was becoming too important to her. While she planned her new life, looking forward to all the exciting things stretching out in front of her, Sage was in those mental images, too. He had become a part of the dream she'd nurtured for so long and she didn't know how to separate them now.

The only thing she *could* do was try to protect her heart from the inevitable crash that was headed her way.

"Hello?" Jenna demanded her attention. "Did you know he was that rich?"

In spite of everything, Colleen laughed. "It never crossed my mind to ask J.D. what Sage's bank account looked like."

"Well, it just doesn't seem fair, does it?" Jenna turned the laptop so that Colleen could see the screen, where an image of Sage stared out at her. "A man should not be allowed to be *that* amazing-looking *and* rich to boot. Just seems selfish somehow."

Colleen would have laughed, but she was staring at the image of Sage, drawn from some tabloid site. He looked impossibly handsome in a tux and was glaring at the camera even as the woman on his arm, last year's Oscar winner, beamed at the photographer as she draped herself against Sage's broad chest.

There it was, she told herself silently. Proof that whatever was between her and Sage wasn't permanent. Wasn't anything more than a temporary fantasy on her part, just a lot of chemistry that sizzled and flashed between them.

So, knowing it was all fleeting, what was she supposed to do? Stay home? Avoid Sage? Or should she accept the fact that this was all transitory and simply enjoy it for what it was? A swirl of expectation swam in her veins, side by side with a few slim threads of reality. It would be interesting to see which sensation finally won out.

"Anyway," Jenna was saying as she slapped the laptop lid down, shattering the spell Colleen had been under. "I found a couple of cabins for sale. One has a lot of land with it—like thirty acres—the other's close to a county road."

"Sounds great." She smiled appreciatively as Jenna handed over a piece of paper with the addresses. "I'll see if Sage can take me to look at them."

"We're depending on Sage a lot lately, aren't we?"

Colleen quirked a smile. "Is that the royal *we?*"

"It's the *you* we," Jenna said, leaning back against the headboard of Colleen's bed and stretching out her legs to cross them at the ankle. "You've really been seeing a lot of him and now you're off to stay with him at his place."

"Not *with* him," Colleen corrected, though her body hummed at the idea. "Just at his house."

"Uh-huh." Jenna just looked at her for a second or two, then she huffed out a breath. "It's crazy, I know, but I'm worried he's going to break your heart."

"What?" Surprised, Colleen stared at her friend.

"Okay, sure, I was caught up in the whole billionaire-suddenly-wanting-to-date-my-friend thing, too. But honestly, now that he's stuck around for a while, I'm just… uneasy."

"Why?" Colleen knew why Jenna was uneasy, of course. Because she still couldn't quite bring herself to believe that Sage was actually interested in her. But she'd like to hear her friend's reasons.

"Because he's too damn solitary," Jenna blurted. "Anybody who's alone *that* much? There's probably a

reason and I don't want to see you get caught up in whatever his issues are."

Colleen laughed shortly.

"What's so funny?" Jenna demanded.

"Nothing." Waving one hand, she said, "It's just, I
thought you were going to say what I've been telling
myself. That I'm not the kind of woman he usually goes
for. Not sophisticated enough or beautiful enough or rich
enough for him."

"Please." Clearly offended, Jenna sat straight up.
"He'd be lucky to have you. You're plenty beautiful and
way better than sophisticated or rich, you're *real*. You
have a warm and generous heart. Maybe sometimes too
generous."

Colleen reached over and hugged Jenna tight. When
she let her go again, she said, "Thanks for that. But don't
worry, okay? I'm pretty sure that whatever this is, it's
short-lived. I'm not going to let my too-generous heart
get all gooey and involved. Honestly."

"You know the too generous thing was a compliment, right?"

"Absolutely."

"Good." Jenna nodded. "So…back to mystery mountain man."

"He's not a mystery," Colleen insisted. "And this
isn't some romantic getaway. Sage is going to show me
around the mountain and probably try to scare me out
of the idea of living alone up there."

"If only he could."

"Thank you for your support," Colleen said wryly.

"Oh, I support you, sweetie." Jenna sat up, grabbed a
T-shirt and folded it as she continued, "But you forget,
I've lived in Wyoming all my life. I know how danger-

ous the mountains can be. Beautiful, yes, but also deadly if you're not careful."

Colleen started to talk, but her friend cut her off.

"I don't like the idea of you living in the high country all on your own." She waved one hand as if to dismiss the argument she didn't give Colleen a chance to make. "Yeah, yeah, feminists, hear us roar, but just because you *can* do a thing doesn't mean you *should* do it, you know?"

Colleen dropped onto the edge of the bed, pushed the suitcase out of the way and faced her friend. "Fine. I'm a little anxious about being alone up there, I admit it, but I'll get used to it. And Jenna, I'm not helpless or stupid. I'll take care and I'll make sure to get help if I need it."

"I know." Jenna nodded and shrugged helplessly. "Maybe I just don't want you to move away."

Colleen leaned in and gave her friend another hug. "I'll miss you, too. But we'll still see each other."

"Oh, you bet we will. You're not going to get rid of me *that* easy." Jenna handed her the folded shirt. "But do me a favor. When you see the cabins, even if you fall in love…don't make a hasty decision. I don't want you to rush into something that you won't be able to get out of easily."

That was good advice. And not just about the cabins. She was about to head off to stay at the home of a man who turned her knees to mush. Was she already in way too deep for her own good? Would she get out now if she could?

No.

Colleen thought about it while she finished packing and realized that if it would be smart to stay far, far away from Sage Lassiter…she'd rather be stupid.

* * *

It had only been a week.

But in that week, Sage had spent a lot of time with Colleen and when he wasn't with her, she was filling his mind. He still wasn't sure how she'd managed it, but whenever they were together, she actually got him to talk. He'd opened up to her about his ranch, his plans, his life—something he hadn't done with anyone else. Not even Dylan or Angelica.

Colleen had slipped up on him. He hadn't expected to actually *like* her. Hadn't thought that he'd want her so badly that every night was a torture and every day was a lesson in self-control. Plus, he was no closer to finding out what he needed to know than he had been before this started.

Was this a deliberate maneuver on her part? Suck him in, distract him with her big blue eyes and then set the sexual tension bar so damn high that he couldn't think straight?

If that was her plan, it was a damn good one.

Hell, he hadn't even *kissed* her. How could he be this torn up and feel so out of control over a woman he hadn't even *kissed?*

"And why haven't you kissed her?" he asked himself in disgust. Because he knew that the moment he tasted her, took that luscious, amazing mouth with his, that there would be no stopping. He'd have to have *all* of her. And that had not been the plan. But then, he'd expected that he would have answers by now. Since this was going to take longer than he'd thought, the plan had to change.

As that thought settled into his mind, Sage took his first easy breath in a week. Talking to her wasn't working, so he would seduce any secrets she held out of her.

He'd use sex—crazed, hot, sweaty, incredible sex—to find out if she was withholding any information he might need to contest the will.

Then when he had what he needed, he would walk away.

She wasn't the kind of woman to go for a one-night stand, and once she discovered that was all he was willing to offer her, she'd *let* him walk.

But first, he would have her. Under him. Over him. And then he'd finally be able to get her out of his mind.

He scrubbed both hands over his face, then adjusted the fit of his jeans, hoping to ease the ache that had locked around his groin for the past week. It didn't help. Nothing would. The only way to ease that pain was to bury himself inside Colleen and thankfully, that was about to happen. He'd felt the chemistry between them. Knew that she was strung as tightly as he was. Seducing her wouldn't be difficult.

She was going to be here. Every day. Every night. He could hear her voice in his mind again: *Will you show me what I need to know?* Oh, there was plenty that he wanted to show her and very little of it had to do with survival.

What the hell had he been thinking, asking her to stay here? "Must be a closet masochist," he muttered darkly.

Or he *had* been, before he'd altered his plan. But things were different now. When Colleen finally showed up here at the house today, he was going to do what he should have done days ago: kiss the hell out of her. And then he'd get her into his bed as quickly as possible and scramble her mind so completely, she'd tell him whatever he needed to know.

Gritting his teeth against yet another wave of desire

thrumming inside him, he turned into the stable and headed down the long center aisle. The familiar scents of horses, straw and leather combined to welcome him and he sighed in gratitude. One thing he could count on was that being with the horses he bred and raised eased his mind. Here, he could push thoughts of Colleen aside—however briefly.

He paused long enough to greet one of the mares who poked her head through the half door to her stall.

"Belle, you're a beauty," he whispered. The chestnut mare butted his shoulder with her head as he stroked her jaw and neck, murmuring soft words that had the animal whickering in delight. It was this he lived for. Being around these animals that he loved. Caring for them, training them. Horses didn't lie. Didn't betray you. They were who they were and you accepted them at face value. You always knew where you stood with an animal.

It was people who let you down.

"Hey, boss!"

Frowning at the interruption, Sage gave the horse one last pat and turned to look back at one of the cowboys who lived on his ranch. "What is it, Pete?"

"Thought you'd like to know your sister just drove up."

Of course she did. Grimacing tightly, Sage muttered, "Okay, thanks."

So much for looking in on the newest foal born on the ranch. Instead, he gave the mare another long stroke over her neck, then headed back out of the stable. Pushing one hand through his hair, he told himself that it seemed women were destined to plague him lately. Wouldn't you know his sister would show up on the very day he was at last going to taste Colleen Falkner?

Sage couldn't even remember the last time Angie had come up the mountain to see him. Hell, usually she was living in L.A., but when she did come home, she stayed at Big Blue and visited her friends in Cheyenne.

But this visit was different, wasn't it? She'd lost her father, and then lost faith in him. She was upset about the will and having lost control of Lassiter Media, he knew. What he didn't know was what he could do about it. He and Dylan had talked this through several times and neither of them had come up with a way to challenge J.D.'s will.

So far, it had been made plain to them all that J.D. had definitely been in his right mind when he had the will drafted, and fighting his last wishes might very well invalidate the whole document. Until they could be sure of their next moves, he and Dylan at least had agreed to take this slowly.

Since J.D. was gone now, that made Sage the head of the family—and he had to consider everyone's inheritances, not just Angie's. He didn't want to risk Chance losing the ranch, or their aunt Marlene losing her bequest.

As much as it pained him, Sage couldn't make this any easier on the sister he loved. All he could really do was listen. A damned helpless feeling for a man more accustomed to having the answers than scrambling unsuccessfully for them. Scrubbing his hands over his face, he pushed those unsettling thoughts from his mind and headed for the main house.

The ranch yard was laid out a lot like Big Blue, he thought as he walked across it. But that wasn't a homage to J.D., he assured himself. It just made sense. The main house was set back at the end of a curving drive.

A landscaped sweep of greenery and flowers spread out in front of it in barely tamed splendor. The barn, stables and cabins for the cowhands who worked and lived on the ranch were set farther back and there was a pool that curved around a rock waterfall, with a stone patio surrounding it.

And from every spot on his property, the views were tremendous. He'd had his architect build the house to accommodate the beauty and become a part of the mountains itself. Acres of wood and glass and stone made the house look as though it had always been there, as if it had grown from the rocks and the forest. Trees were everywhere, and the scent of pine flavored every breath.

In Wyoming, winter held on, sometimes even into summer, especially this high up the mountain. An icy wind tore at Sage's hair as he walked toward his sister. Angelica was just climbing out of her car when he approached, and one look at her told Sage that she wasn't in much better shape than she had been when he'd seen her a couple nights ago.

True to their plan, he and Dylan had dropped in on their sister at Big Blue. It still wasn't easy walking into that house, cluttered with memories, but for his sister, he was willing to bite the bullet.

Evan had been there too, of course, but the tension between the formerly happy couple was unmistakable. Evan was doing his best to make this work, but Angie was so hurt and angry at her father that there wasn't a lot of give in her at the moment. How they were managing to work together through this was a mystery to Sage. Judging by the tight expression on Angie's face now, that tension hadn't eased up any either.

"Sorry to just drop in," she blurted, shrugging into

a navy blue sweater that dropped to midthigh. "I had to get out of the house."

"You're welcome here anytime," Sage told her, mentally letting go of his plans for Colleen—at least until his sister was on her way again. "What's going on now?"

"What *isn't?*" she snapped, then stopped, gave him a sheepish look and said, "I'm sorry, Sage. Seriously, I'm acting like queen bitch of the universe and I can't seem to stop myself."

"Hey," he said, dropping one arm around her shoulder and pulling her in for a hug, "that's my baby sister you're talking about."

Angie wrapped both arms around his waist and held on. Tenderness swamped Sage as he simply stood there holding her, knowing there was nothing he could say to make things better. Since she was a little girl, Sage had done everything he could to protect her. To take care of her. He hated not being able to help her now.

After a long minute or two, she pulled back and looked up at him. "You always steady me. How do you do that?"

"It's a gift," he quipped and gave her another squeeze. "Now, you want to fill me in on what's happening?"

She leaned into him. "It's just a rumor."

"Plenty of them to go around," Sage said, giving her a squeeze. "Tell me what you heard."

Tipping her head back, she looked up at him and bit her lip. Then she finally blurted, "The word is, Jack Reed is interested in Lassiter Media."

Jack Reed. Sage wasn't really surprised…how could he be? Jack Reed had the reputation of a great white shark. He bought up companies in trouble, then broke them down to the bare bones and sold off the pieces.

If Reed was interested, then it wouldn't be long before more sharks started circling the Lassiter family. They couldn't afford to be divided right now. They had to stand together against all comers. Which was just what he told Angie.

"We *are* together," she argued.

"What we are is pissed," he said flatly. "We all are. And we're spending too damn much time trying to figure out what was running through J.D.'s mind when he made that will."

"I know, I know." She stepped away from him, pulled the edges of her sweater tighter and wrapped her arms around her middle. "My first instinct, you know, was to contest the will."

"Yeah, I felt the same way," he said, "so did Dylan." He didn't add that he and their brother hadn't been able to come to a decision.

She took a deep breath and tossed her hair back from her face. "I don't know what the right thing to do is anymore, Sage. I want that company, but now I don't know how to get it. Do I fight my father's dying wishes? Do I try to accept this? How?"

"The whole situation's screwed up, that's for damn sure. But we'll figure something out," Sage said. He knew what J.D. had done had eaten away at her confidence, her self-assurance—hell, even her own image of herself. Their dad had spent a lifetime building her up and then with one stroke of the pen, he'd torn her down.

Why?

She laughed shortly and threw both hands into the air. "I'm a mess, sorry. I shouldn't have just driven up here and thrown myself on you. But I really needed someone to talk to. Someone who would understand."

"You can drop in on me any damn time you want and you know that, Angie," he told her. "But just out of curiosity, where's Marlene?"

"Oh, she's at the ranch," she said, and started walking toward the wraparound porch on the main house. Sage matched his strides to her shorter ones. "And yes, she's always willing to listen, but she can't be objective about Dad...and I really wish Colleen were still at Big Blue. She was super easy to talk to."

Yeah, he thought. Colleen was easy to talk to. Easy to look at. She also made it easy for him to forget why he'd started all of this.

As if just thinking about her could make her appear, an old red Jeep pulled up the drive and everything in Sage quickened. Like a damn kid waiting for a date with the girl of his dreams, he felt his heartbeat thundering in his chest, and an all-too-familiar ache settled low in his gut and grabbed hold.

"Well," Angie said thoughtfully, with a pointed glance at him. "This is interesting."

Instantly, Sage tamped down the internal fires raging through him. He didn't need his sister making more of this than there was. "It's not what you're thinking, so dial it down."

"Really?" she asked as the car engine cut off and the driver's side door opened. "Because that looks like a suitcase she's pulling out of her car...."

His insides tightened even further. "Don't even start, Angie...."

Colleen wrangled her overnight bag out of the car and set it at her feet. She looked at the ranch house and quickly swept it in one thorough gaze. It was smaller than Big Blue, but not by much. Its windows gleamed in the afternoon sun and the long wraparound porch boasted plenty of chairs for sitting out and enjoying the view. The honey-colored logs looked warm and inviting, the scent of pine was pervasive, and the two people on the porch were both watching her.

She hadn't expected to find Sage's sister here, too, but maybe that was a good thing. All morning, Colleen's stomach had been twisting and turning in anticipation of her arrival here at Sage's ranch. For longer than she cared to think about she had been fascinated by him. And now that they'd actually been spending time together, that fascination had escalated into something that was as scary as it was thrilling. Having Angie as a buffer might make these first few minutes easier.

"Angie, hi." Though she spoke to his sister, Colleen's gaze went first to Sage, and even that one brief connection with his intense blue eyes sent goose bumps racing along her spine.

"Hi, yourself." Angelica walked out to meet her and gave Colleen a hug. "I've missed you since you moved out of Big Blue."

"I missed you, too." Focusing on his sister gave Colleen the chance to tear her gaze from Sage's. "How is everyone doing? Marlene?"

"She really misses Dad. A lot. We all do, of course, but…" Angie shrugged. "It's hard. And since the reading of the will, it's even harder." Taking a deep breath, she looked up at Sage. "Why don't you get Colleen's suitcase and I'll walk her in."

"Oh, that's okay, I can—"

Sage nudged her hand off the handle, and a now-familiar buzz of sensation hummed from her fingers, up her arm, to rocket around in the center of her chest.

He looked at her, and in his eyes, she saw the realization that he'd felt it, too. That electric spark that happened whenever they touched. As if a match had been held to a slow burning fuse that was about to reach the explosives it was attached to.

Then he picked up her suitcase as if it weighed nothing—and Colleen knew she hadn't packed light. For another long second, he looked at her and Colleen's heart beat began to race. Her mouth went dry, her knees went weak and if Angie hadn't been there, watching the two of them, she might have just thrown herself at Sage.

"Come on," Angie said then, splintering that happy little fantasy. Colleen followed her into the house and once she was there, she buried those feelings in the curiosity she had for Sage's ranch. She'd heard J.D. describe it, of course, but the reality was so much more.

Outside, it was set up much like the Big Blue. Outbuildings, barns, stables, though from what she'd seen at a quick glance, there was a much bigger corral for working horses than J.D.'s ranch provided. Obviously, that made sense, because she knew that Sage bred and raised racehorses. But it was the *inside* of the main house that had her captivated.

It, too, was constructed of hand-hewn logs, but there the similarity with Big Blue ended. Instead of the ironwork that made up much of the Lassiter home ranch, Sage's place was all wood and glass. Wood banisters on the wide staircase, intricately carved to look like vines climbing up posts. Bookcases that looked as though they'd been sculpted into the walls, boasted hundreds of leather-bound and paperback books.

The wide front windows afforded a view that was so spectacular it took her breath away. Despite the number of trees on the property, the view was wide-open and provided a glimpse of the valley and the city of Cheyenne that at night must be staggering. A stone fireplace dominated one wall and the hand-carved mantel displayed pictures of his brother and sister and a young couple who must have been his biological parents.

While Sage and Angie talked, their conversation veering from muted tones to half shouts, Colleen wandered around the great room. Oak floorboards shone in the sunlight slanting through the windows. Brightly colored rugs dotted the floor, adding more warmth to a room that rang with comfort. Overstuffed brown leather chairs and sofas were gathered in conversational knots and heavy oak tables were laden with yet more stacks of books. She loved it.

The house was perfect and she couldn't wait to explore the rest of it. It was just as she would like her own home to be—on a smaller scale, of course. A comfortable refuge.

"You don't understand," Angie was saying and had Colleen turning around to face the siblings. "Evan is acting as if this is nothing. He keeps offering to let me run the company. But he doesn't get that him *giving* me control isn't the same as *having* control. He's trying to take a step back for me at the office, but I don't want him doing that, so it's a vicious circle. He thinks I should have control, and I want it, but if Dad *didn't* want me to have it, how can I try to claim it? We're arguing all the time now, and I can't help wondering why Dad did this. Did he want Evan and I to break up? Or was he really that disappointed in me?"

Colleen saw the torment on Sage's face and when he reached for his sister, pulling her in tight and wrapping his arms around her, Colleen felt a pang in her tender heart. He was so kind. So loving. Yet when she'd told him just that, he'd denied it. Why couldn't he see it?

"Dad loved you," he said simply. "Something else is going on here, Angie, and we will find out what it is."

His gaze speared into Colleen's and she felt a quick bolt of ice that snaked along her spine and made her shiver. There was nothing tender in that look. But before she could really wonder what he was thinking, the expression dissolved once again into concern for his sister.

Angie pulled away, spun around and looked at Colleen. "You're the one who spent the most time with him toward the end. Did he tell you why he was doing this? Why he cut me out as if I were nothing?"

With both Lassiters staring at her, Colleen felt completely ill at ease. She didn't have answers for them, though she wished she had.

Shaking her head, she could only say, "No, Angie. He didn't talk about his will with me. I had no idea what he was going to bequeath to everyone."

"That's really not an answer though, is it?" Sage muttered and her gaze locked on his. The shutters were in place, but even with him closing her out, she felt the cold emanating from him. Only minutes ago, he'd given her a look filled with heat, and now it was as if he'd shut that part of himself down.

"He talked to you, Colleen," he prodded. "If not about his will, then about how he was feeling. What he was thinking. And you know what he said. So tell us."

She blinked at him. "What can I tell you that you don't already know? He loved you all. He talked about you with such warmth. So much pride…"

"Then why would he do this?" Angie demanded. *"Why?"*

"I just don't know." Colleen sighed heavily. "I wish I did."

Sage's features went very still, as if he were considering what she said and wondering if she was holding something back. Finally he muttered, "Angie, she doesn't know. No one does. *Yet.* We'll find out, though, I swear."

"For all the good it'll do," she said and forced a smile. "I'm really sorry. I don't mean to dump on you guys. I'm just so torn up about this and so...*confused.*"

"Your father loved you, Angie," Colleen said softly. "He was proud of you."

Her eyes glistened with tears, but she blinked them back and lifted her chin. "I want to believe you, Colleen. I really do."

"You can."

"I hope so." Nodding, she turned to her brother. "I'm gonna go. I promised Marlene I'd take her into town for a nice dinner, and if I'm going to make it, I've got to start back now."

"Okay," Sage said, dropping a kiss on her forehead. "Try not to worry. We'll work this out."

"Sure." She flashed a smile at Colleen. "And now, I can leave you two alone to do...whatever you were planning before I showed up."

Colleen flushed. "Oh, please don't get the wrong idea. I'm just here so Sage can show me what life in the mountains is like. I want to move up here and—"

"You're going to move here?" Angie interrupted.

"Not *here,* here," Colleen corrected with a fast glance at Sage to see what his reaction was to his sister's teasing. But it was as if he wasn't listening to Angie at all.

His gaze was locked with hers and the heat in his eyes warmed her all the way to her toes. Still, she added for Angie's benefit, "Just here in the mountains, here."

She was babbling and now felt like an idiot. Of course Angie hadn't meant anything by what she'd said. She knew that there was nothing between Colleen and Sage. Nothing but a lot of chemistry that neither of them had acted on.

"Right, so you have a place in mind?"

"I have the addresses of a couple of cabins that are for sale. I was hoping Sage could show me where they are."

"Oh, my big brother is so *helpful,* I'm sure he won't mind at all." She smiled at him. "Will you, Sage?"

"Don't you have somewhere to be?" he asked pointedly.

Brother and sister stared at each other for a long minute or two, then finally Angie said, "Yeah. I guess I do. After dinner with Marlene, I'm meeting Evan in town tonight. We both thought it would be better to talk away from the office. It's just too…hard when we're there. But we do have to talk about plans for the company."

"That's good, Angie."

"In theory," she said. "We'll have to see, now that he's my *boss.*"

Colleen winced and wished she knew why J.D. had done this to his daughter. She would love to be able to give Angie a reason. An explanation. Something. But she simply had no idea why he would turn his family on its head like he had. And she couldn't help but feel guilty every time she thought about what Angelica was going through. She'd been hurt by her father's will while Colleen had been given a gift for which she was immensely grateful.

"Anyway," Angie said, crossing the room to hug Colleen. "You guys have fun or whatever. Don't let him turn you into Dan'l Boone or something, okay?"

Colleen laughed. "I don't think that's going to be an issue."

"You never know when the hermit of the mountain's involved."

"'Bye, Angie," Sage said firmly.

"Uh-huh." Angie shifted a sly look between the two of them then flashed a knowing smile at Colleen. "I'm sure Sage will show you *everything* you'll ever need to know."

And with that loaded insinuation, she left, Sage walking her out. Alone in the great room, Colleen found herself suddenly wondering if the lessons she came to learn weren't going to be very different than what she'd expected.

Eight

Once his sister was gone, Sage went back into the house and stopped in the doorway of the great room. Colleen had her back to him as she stared out the windows at the wide, uninterrupted view of trees and sky. His gaze raked her up and down and his body roared into life in response.

Hell, he'd been with beautiful, glamorous women who spent hours in front of mirrors, and had their own fashion stylists, hair people, makeup artists, and he'd never felt the pulse-pounding desire for them that he did for Colleen. Her hair was loose, hanging over her shoulders in a windblown tousle of waves and curls. She wore jeans, sneakers and a red sweater over a white shirt. And she looked amazing.

As if sensing his presence, she turned to face him and their eyes locked.

"I feel really bad about all of this will business," she said, her soft voice barely discernible in the cavernous room.

A brief spark of suspicion rose up inside him. Was she going to confess to conspiring with J.D. to cheat Angie out of what was rightfully hers? Hell, he almost hoped not, because he *really* wanted to seduce it out of her. "Why should you?"

"I know how upset she is over the will…and yet for me, it was life changing."

"For her, too," Sage said wryly.

She winced. "I know. I wish I could help."

With the afternoon sunlight streaming in through the window behind her, Colleen looked as though the tips of her hair were dusted with gold. She seemed to shimmer in that soft light and damned if he didn't feel that lurch of something that was more than attraction. More than simple desire.

Shaking his head, he asked, "You actually mean that, don't you?"

"Of course I mean it," she said, clearly confused by the question. "Why wouldn't I?"

Why indeed. If she was hiding something, she was damn good at it. And if she was innocent—that didn't change anything. He still wanted her and he would still *have* her.

"Never mind," he said, walking toward her in long, easy strides. "Let me see the addresses of those cabins."

She dug the paper out of her pocket and handed it over. He knew both places. One wasn't far. The other was much higher up the mountain. "Okay, let's go take a look."

* * *

"This is Ed Jackson's place," Sage said as he steered Colleen down the rocky path toward the small one-bedroom cabin. The first address she'd given him was about two miles higher up the mountain from Sage's ranch. The roads were in good repair, but the sharp curves and the straight-down drop off the edge were enough to give even the best drivers nightmares.

And he hadn't missed the fact that Colleen had had a death grip on the armrest every time he maneuvered around one of those curves that had been carved out of the mountain. But now that they'd arrived, the look on her face told him that she was so entranced by the setting she'd already forgotten the treacherous ride to get there. He held on to her hand as they took the narrow path to the front door, relishing the buzz of sensation that simply touching her caused.

The flower beds had long ago gone to seed and now there were only monstrous weeds fighting each other for space. The cabin itself was well built, but the white paint on the wood-plank walls was cracked and peeling. The front porch still boasted two chairs, and he remembered coming up here as a kid to find Ed and his wife sitting side by side, talking and laughing together. But then Helen had died five years ago and Ed lived here alone, refusing to move to the city. Finally, though, age had conquered his stubbornness, forcing him to put the home he loved up for sale and move to an assisted-living apartment in Cheyenne.

"It's pretty," she said, stopping to take it all in. "I love all the trees standing like guarding sentries around it."

"Nice spot," he agreed, trying to keep his mind off the

fact that she was close enough to touch. Close enough to— "Come on. I'll show you the inside."

"We can get in?"

"Ed always left a key above the doorframe." He found it, unlocked the front door and stepped into the past. The furnishings were at least forty years old and the air smelled of neglect and loneliness.

He watched as Colleen walked through the small house, checking out the tiny bedroom, the single bath and then the functional but narrow kitchen. Every window sported a view of the surrounding forest and the deep ravine that tracked off to one side of the house. "Why's the owner selling?"

He told her Ed's story and watched as sympathy filled her eyes. She was intriguing. Always. He liked that she cared why a house was for sale and that she felt pity for the man forced by time to give up the house he loved. He felt a swift stab of something beyond the pulsing desire still throbbing inside him, but he ignored it and looked at the cabin through objective eyes.

"You'd have to get a generator," he said, scanning the interior. "Ed didn't care about losing power, but I'm thinking you would."

She smiled and his heart rate jumped into a gallop. "You're right."

"You've got a wood-burning stove, so that's good," he continued, slapping one hand down on the dusty cast-iron fireplace in one corner of the living room. "But those pines along the side of the house will have to be cut way back or down altogether. Too dangerous. A heavy snowfall or a high wind could bring them crashing down on your roof. Not to mention, you should have a clearing around the house in case of forest fires."

"But those trees have been there for *years*."

"Yeah, Ed wasn't worried about the *what-ifs,* because he could patch a roof or get out there and hack out a clearing fast if he needed to." He paused meaningfully. "You couldn't."

She frowned slightly, walking through the room, running her fingertips across the backs of the chairs, straightening framed photographs on the walls.

"Structure's sound enough, I guess," he mused, looking around in an effort to keep from staring at her. "But you'd have to have an inspection to be sure. County road's at the end of the drive, so the snow would get cleared fairly quickly out there."

She glanced at him. "What about the drive itself?"

He looked at her then and shook his head. "The county's not going to clear your drive. You'd have to get a snowblower or hire someone to come in after a storm."

Colleen nodded and huffed out a breath as she considered everything he was saying. She was getting a hard lesson in what it meant to live so far from the city, and he almost felt sorry for her. Almost, but not quite, because he still didn't like the idea of her being up here on her own. There were women on this mountain capable of taking care of any kind of emergency, and he knew that. But Colleen was city through and through, and she had no idea of what she might be letting herself in for.

"You'll want the roof checked out, too," he added. "We had heavy snows last winter and Ed wasn't in shape to take care of things like that himself."

"Right. Another inspection," she murmured, looking around the room wistfully.

"This lot's on high ground, so you don't have to worry too much about spring runoff, but you should have the gullies cleared so melting snow won't get backed up and flood the house."

She laughed a little. "So I have to worry about the snowfall and then about when the snow melts."

"Pretty much." He leaned against one wall and watched as she peered through the kitchen window at the surrounding trees.

"How long did Ed and his wife live here?"

"About forty years," he said with a shrug. "After Helen died, Ed didn't visit much with anyone. They never had kids—it was always just the two of them. And without her, he kept to himself. Didn't really keep up with the cabin, either."

"He missed her." She turned to look at him.

Gaze locked with hers, he nodded. "Yeah, he did."

Which was yet another reason to keep to yourself. If you never let anyone in, you didn't miss them when they were gone. He'd learned that lesson as a kid—and then again later on, when he should have known better, but took a risk, only to be slammed for it.

"I want to look around outside," she said and he wondered if she could read minds. She was staring at him oddly and she'd suddenly gone quiet, and that just wasn't like Colleen.

But he followed her out, locked the door after them and returned the key to its resting place. She walked to the end of the porch, leaned on the railing and gazed out over the rocky ravine that dropped from the edge of the porch and ran down the side of the mountain. Her hair trailed over her shoulders and as she leaned out farther, her jeans tightened over her behind, making Sage's breathing a hell of a lot harder to control.

Then everything changed.

He heard a snap, then a squeak of alarm, and he was moving before he even realized it. In a blink, he reached out and caught her arm as the railing gave way. He heard the crash and rattle as the heavy wood barrier, rotted by time and weather, clattered and rolled down into the rocks below.

Pulling Colleen tight against him, he wrapped both arms around her and held on. He felt her trembling and knew that he was doing the same damn thing. "I told you he hadn't kept the place up." His voice came out in a harsh rasp of tension and what felt a lot like fear. "Never lean on a railing you're not sure about. Hell. Never lean on a railing no matter what."

"Good advice," she murmured, her voice muffled against his chest. When she lifted her head and looked up at him, Sage felt the last of his control snap as completely as that rotted-out railing had.

Her mouth was *right there*. Her breathing was fast and the pulse point in her throat throbbed. He knew she was shaken. So was he. If he hadn't grabbed her so quickly, she might now be at the bottom of that damned ravine. Broken. Bleeding. Hell, she'd have been lucky to survive the fall.

But she hadn't fallen. And now she was pressed close to him and when his control snapped, all he could think was *thank God*. He bent his head, covered her mouth with his and tasted her for the first time.

Heat slammed into him and Sage surrendered to it. His kiss was hard and fierce and desperate. No time for subtle seduction. This was need. Hot and thick and running through his body like lava. He ground his mouth over hers and felt her surrender when she lifted her arms to wrap them around his neck.

He groaned in response and flipped them around until her back was braced against the cabin wall. His tongue parted her lips and he delved deep, determined to taste all of her after waiting so long. Longer than he'd ever waited before to claim a woman he desired. And he'd never wanted a woman as he wanted Colleen.

Fire roared through his veins, blurring his mind, leaving only his body in charge, and the aching throb in his groin let him know he couldn't wait much longer. Need pounded inside him, feeding the flames threatening to consume him. Her breasts pressed to his chest, her fingers sliding up into his hair and all he could think was *too many clothes.*

The icy-cold wind sliding off the top of the mountain didn't deter him as he reached down and tugged the hem of her shirt up. She shivered, but continued kissing him, giving him everything she had, pouring her own need and desire into the melding of their mouths.

His hands cupped her breasts and she gasped, tearing her mouth from his to lean her head back against the cabin wall and arch her body into his touch. Even through the fragile lace of her bra, he thumbed her nipples until she was groaning, leaning into him, offering herself.

And he took. Lifting the bra up and out of his way, Sage looked his fill of the full, luscious breasts that he hadn't been able to stop thinking about since the first night he'd seen her in that red dress. Her dusky-rose nipples were hard and erect and he couldn't help himself. He dipped low and took first one, then the other into his mouth, rolling that sensitive tip between his lips and tongue, scraping the edges of his teeth across the pebbly surface until she was sobbing his name. She held his head to her tightly and when he suckled her she actually shrieked. That unfettered sound went straight to his groin and pushed him to take more. To give more.

To have it all.

He straightened up, dropped his hands to the waistband of her jeans and quickly undid the snap and zipper. Their eyes were locked on each other as he dipped one hand down, sliding across her abdomen, beneath the sliver of elastic of the panties she wore, and then delved deeper, cupping her hot, wet core. At his first touch, her so-expressive eyes glazed over and she rocked her hips into his hand, silently asking for more. But he held still, not moving, not stroking, torturing them both. He luxuriated in the feel of her hot, slick flesh beneath his hand and gritted his teeth as he fought for control. Then he slid the pad of his thumb across one particularly sensitive spot and her body jerked in response.

Her breath hissed in and out of her lungs, her eyes grew wide, her lips parted and her tongue swept out to lick them. He bent his head and kissed her briefly as he continued to tease her, stroking that bud of sensation, enjoying the tremors that continued to rack her body as she twisted and writhed in his grasp.

"Sage, please…" She tore her mouth from his to beg him for the release he continued to keep just out of her reach. "You have to," she murmured, her gaze imploring him, pleading with him to ease the coiled tension inside her. "Touch me. Take me."

He lost himself in her eyes and gave her what she needed. What they *both* needed. Sage dipped his fingers into her depths, stroking, caressing. Her movements quickened, her breath was strangled, and still she whispered his name as the cold air wrapped itself around them in an icy embrace. He felt the magic of her tight heat as she groaned and writhed wildly against him. She clung to his shoulders, widened her stance to give him more access and moved with him at every stroke of his hand.

He watched her. Couldn't take his eyes off of her. He'd never seen anything more beautiful than Colleen in the grip of passion. Small, breathless sounds escaped her throat. She chewed at her bottom lip and locked her gaze with his until all he could see of the world were her amazing, deep blue eyes.

Everything she felt shone clearly on her face, so he knew when her climax was hurtling toward her. Knew when she reached the precipice and fused his mouth to hers when she finally bolted over the edge, trembling and quaking in his arms with the force of her release.

And when it was done, he wanted more. He was hungrier for her now than he had been before he had touched her, and damned if he was going to wait any longer.

"Come with me," he blurted, hoping she could hear him through the sexual haze clouding her mind and her eyes.

He didn't bother doing up her jeans again. He'd only have to undo them in a second or two. Taking hold of her hand, he marched back to the front door, grabbed the key and unlocked it. Pulling her inside after him, he threw the bolt on the door, then grabbed her and held her tightly enough to him that she couldn't help but feel the hard thickness of his own arousal pushing into her. Still, she was a little nervous about going into someone else's home like this.

"Can we do this? In a stranger's house?"

"Ed's not a stranger to me," Sage whispered. "Trust me, he'd approve. So? What do you think?"

Colleen hoped he was right about what Ed would think because she really didn't want to waste this moment. He was staring down into her eyes and her sense of caution was washed away in a rising tide of desire.

"Yes," she whispered in answer to his unspoken question. "Yes, Sage. Now."

She licked her lips and then went up on her toes to kiss him as hungrily as he had kissed her the first time. He met that passion with all of his own. Tearing her sweater off, he then pulled up her shirt and whipped it over her head before tossing it to the nearest chair. She was pulling at his jacket, too, then ripping at his shirt. He heard a couple of buttons sail across the room and he didn't give a damn. Anything to have her skin against his. Now. This minute.

No more waiting.

He was blind to everything but her. Sage had never known such all-consuming desire before. Sex had always been fast and hot and no deeper than a puddle. This was more because *she* was more. But he didn't want to think about that now. Didn't want to consider just *why* he was so desperate to have her. It was enough that he needed. Wanted.

She pulled free of the kiss, reached for his belt buckle and undid it, her gaze on his, never shifting. *Nothing sexier than a woman who can look you in the eye while getting naked.* She unbuttoned his jeans and then reached inside to cup her hand around his aching, rock-hard erection.

At the first touch of her fingers, he damn near lost it and that was humiliating to admit, even to himself. But he was wound so tight, hurting so bad, it wasn't surprising. Her grip was strong and gentle, firm and soft, and the touch of her fingers on his sensitized skin was like putting a match to dry kindling.

"Don't." Gritting his teeth, he took hold of her hand and pulled it free as he gave her a half smile to take the sting out of his sharp warning. "You keep that up, and it's over before we get started."

"Okay then. Can't have that." She toed off her sneakers before taking hold of her jeans to drag them off.

"I'll do that," he said, stroking his hands across her breasts, cupping them in his palms, thumbing her nipples, until she swayed unsteadily on her feet. "I've been thinking of nothing but stripping you out of your jeans for the past few days. I want to enjoy the moment."

"Hope it's okay if I enjoy it, too," she whispered.

"Absolutely." Smiling, he dropped his hands to the waist of her jeans and slowly pushed them down over her generous, gorgeous hips. He took that tiny swatch of lace panties with him as he went, and going down on his knees, he left a trail of kisses along her flesh as it was exposed to his gaze. "You have an amazing body," he murmured.

She squirmed in his grasp and reached down to slide her fingers through his hair, dragging her nails across his scalp. "My boobs are too big," she argued in a quiet voice. "And so are my feet and my butt."

"You're wrong," he whispered and as if to prove a point, he slid his hands around to cup her behind, his fingers kneading her tender flesh until she whimpered and swayed unsteadily. "You have a great butt and your breasts…beautiful."

She held on to his shoulders to keep herself steady

and then stepped out of her jeans when he wanted her to. Then she was naked, standing there in a splash of watery sunlight, as glorious as he'd known she would be. He ran his hands over the line of her hips and all the way down her long, shapely legs to her narrow feet. "I love your curves. A man could get lost in your body and happily stay that way."

She cupped her hand under his chin and tipped his head back so she could look into his eyes. "You mean that," she asked after a long second or two, "don't you?"

"Babe," he assured her, "your body is a wonderland."

She had curves and he liked them. She had long legs and he wanted them wrapped around his hips, pulling him deeper into her body. And the dark blond curls at her center were at just the right height for him to do something he'd been dreaming of doing for far too long.

Still looking up at her, Sage reached out to brush those curls aside, clearing a path for his mouth, his tongue. She knew what he was about to do. Her eyes went wide and she sucked in a deep breath and held it. "Sage…"

"I want to taste all of you," he said and leaned in, covering her heat with his mouth.

She gasped and arched into him, her fingers digging into his shoulders, her short, neat nails scraping his skin. She wobbled unsteadily, but his hands on her butt kept her still, held her in place.

He licked and kissed and stroked and fed the frenzy leaping inside him. He sensed the tension in her body and tightened it with every slide of his tongue. His hands ran up and down her thighs, over her hips, and then dipped down so that he could invade her heat even while he tasted her.

The world shrank down until there was only Colleen. Her taste, her scent—she was all. She was everything. Every soft moan and gasp that escaped from her throat made him more frantic to feel her body bucking under his. He sensed she was close to another climax, and this time, he was going to be buried deep inside her when she came.

And suddenly he couldn't wait another second to bring them together in the only way that mattered. He pulled away, stripped off his jeans and laid her down on the threadbare rug with its pattern of faded pastel flowers. He levered himself over her as she reached for him, parting her legs, so ready, so eager, so—

"Damn it."

"What?" She shook her head, blindly blinking to bring him into focus. "What is it? Why'd you stop? Please, don't stop."

He dropped his forehead to hers and if he'd been strong enough, he would have jumped to his feet and kicked himself. But hell, he hadn't carried protection around with him in the hopes of getting lucky since he was a kid. "Have to stop. No condom."

"No problem."

He lifted his head, stared down into her eyes and asked, "You're covered?"

She licked her lips again, driving him further along the road of no return. "I am. I went on the pill a couple of months ago to regulate my period. As long as you're healthy, we're covered."

Relief flooded him along with a renewed pulse of desire that damn near strangled him. "I'm so healthy I should be two people."

She choked out a laugh. "I only need one of you at the moment."

He grinned. Hell, he'd never talked with a woman once he had her naked. He'd never joked with one, either. Colleen was different on so many levels from every other woman he'd ever known. There was another hard lurch in his chest as his heart thudded like a jackhammer. He wasn't going to examine anything here. Now wasn't the time for thinking—it was just about feeling.

"That's what you're gonna get, babe," he promised and moved to cover her body with his.

Finally, skin to skin. The soft smoothness of her flesh sang against his. Her breasts rose and fell with the quickness of her breath and she lifted one leg to stroke her foot along his calf. Sensations coursed through him, too fast and too many to count. And he didn't need to. Didn't need to worry about a damn thing but getting where he needed to be.

He eased back on his haunches, looked down at her and spread her wide. Stroking her core with his fingertips, he smiled as she twitched and writhed before him, as frantic, as desperate as he.

"Sage, don't make me wait anymore." She lifted her hips in invitation and offered a weak smile. "If you're not inside me soon, I may explode."

"Can't have that," he said, and leaned over her, pushing his body into hers in one swift, sure stroke.

"Sage!" She arched up off the floor at his invasion and he held perfectly still, though it cost him, until she began to adjust to the size of him. Once she had, she moved, lifting her hips, taking him deeper. That provocation was all he needed. He moved against her, his hips rocking, settling into a fast, hard rhythm that she matched. Breaths mingled, kisses lingered, as bodies raced along the line of tension stretched so tautly between them. Hands explored, whispered words lifted into the silence, and the sighs and groans of two bodies merging became a kind of music.

Sage felt surrounded by her, engulfed by her, and he'd never known anything quite like it. Her slick heat held him, her body welcomed him and her hands left trails of fire along his skin wherever she touched him.

Again and again, they parted and came together, each of them eager for the climax just out of reach. Each of them trying to draw out the moment. His mind raced, his heartbeat thrummed in his ears. She locked her incredible legs around his hips and called his name out as the first wave of tremors crashed down on her. He felt every one of them and took her mouth in a hard, deep kiss, swallowing her cries, her breath, everything he could, drawing her into him in every way possible.

And then he let himself follow. Finally surrendering his slippery grip on control, he tumbled off the edge of the world and felt her arms come around him to cushion his fall.

Colleen didn't want to move. Ever. She'd be happy here, forever, just like this, on the hard floor with Sage's muscular body covering hers. She felt alive in a way she never had before. It was as if her entire body had suddenly awakened from a deep sleep. Her heartbeat slowly returned to normal even as she still shook with the force of the release she'd found with Sage.

And already, one pesky corner of her mind was springing into life trying to quantify what had just happened. Trying to explain the unexplainable.

She wasn't a virgin. She'd had sex exactly twice before this time, and looking back, she had to admit that neither of those times had come even *close* to what she'd just experienced.

In fact, it wasn't very long ago that Colleen had decided she simply wasn't a very sexual person. That maybe she was one of those people who would *never* see fireworks or feel the earth move during sex.

Well, she told herself with a self-satisfied grin, so much for *that* theory.

Sage eased up onto one elbow, and instantly, she missed the feeling of him lying atop her. "You okay?"

"Oh, yeah," she said on a sigh. "I'm terrific. You?"

He laughed shortly. "I think so. Come on, that floor can't be too comfortable."

"I'd rather stay here until my legs work again, thanks."

He shook his head and gave her an all-too-brief smile. "I think that's the nicest thing any woman's ever said to me."

And there had no doubt been plenty of them, Colleen thought sadly. The sophisticates. The skinny women with tiny feet in designer shoes. Ah, yes. Well, that thought was enough to put a damper on the lovely residual heat spreading inside, and have her moving to sit up and grab for her clothes.

"So," Sage asked as he, too, got dressed, "what do you think of the cabin?"

She looked up at him and found his eyes unshuttered, filled with a warmth she hadn't seen before. "I like it. Well, everything except the railing." She grimaced. "I didn't even thank you for saving me from that drop."

"I think," he said, "we pretty much thanked each other."

How funny. He'd saved her but couldn't accept her gratitude. As if by keeping an emotional distance, he could compartmentalize what had just happened between them. Which was enough to have Colleen drawing her romantic notions to a quick close.

"Actually, I'm feeling pretty fond of that railing myself," he said, and stood up to tug on his jeans. "If it hadn't snapped…"

She shivered at the thought, remembering the view of the steep drop. Of that moment of sheer terror when she'd thought she was going to fall. Of feeling Sage grab her, pull her in tight and then…

"Hey, Colleen," he said softly. "You okay?"

"Oh, I'm better than okay," she assured him and hoped he didn't hear the tremor in her voice. She was so not okay. She was in turmoil. Because she had just realized that tumbling down a rocky ravine might have bruised and broken her body—but sex with Sage Lassiter just might break her heart.

Nine

He scowled a little. "You surprise me all the damn time."

"That's a bad thing?"

"I don't know yet," he said. He looked down at her as if trying to read her mind, see into her heart. And Colleen really hoped he couldn't. Because right now, he'd see too much. Know too much.

Frowning slightly, he turned his head, glanced out the window and abruptly said, "We have to go. It's snowing."

"Snowing?"

"A spring snow is nothing new, you know that." Sage turned to her and there was a grim expression on his face. "This high up, it's even more likely to happen."

Colleen looked, too, watching as huge white flakes drifted from a cloud-studded sky. An hour ago, it had been cold and clear. But weather in Wyoming was unpredictable at the best of times, as she already knew. When she and her mother had first moved here from California, the first thing they'd learned was, if you don't like the weather, wait five minutes. These few flakes could wink out of existence in minutes—or they could be the herald of a heavy storm. There was just no way to tell.

In a few minutes, they were dressed and leaving the cabin behind. They walked to the car in silence, and on the way down the wickedly winding road, that silence stretched on. Colleen's mind whirled with too many thoughts to sort through. Besides, the silence was deafening and she had to wonder if Sage was regretting what had happened. If he planned to just pretend it *hadn't* happened at all. Maybe it would be better if she pretended the same thing. Heck, if her body wasn't still alive with sensation, Colleen might have been able to believe it.

How could he shut down so completely? Moments ago, there had been heat and wonder and something… *more* between them. And now it was as if he'd already moved on. There was no closeness between them. No sense of extended intimacy.

There was only the softly falling snow.

And the quiet.

By the next morning, Sage had convinced himself that he had overreacted to what had happened the day before.

That long ride from the cabin back to his home ranch had been a tension-filled misery. He'd felt her waiting for him to say something, but what the hell could he say? He'd just thrown her down onto a dirty cabin floor and taken her so fast and so hard she'd probably have bruises. It had been damned humiliating to know how completely he'd lost control. To know that she'd taken him to the edge and then pushed him over. So what the hell could they possibly have talked about?

The storm had faded away soon after they returned to his ranch, leaving just a chill in the air and a few patchy spots of quickly melting snow. He'd needed some space. Some time to get his head together, so he'd ordered up an early dinner, showed Colleen to a room just down the hall from his and said good-night.

He'd seen the flash of surprise in her eyes when he walked away, but he'd had to. If he'd stayed another minute he'd have found a way to tip her back onto the guest-room bed and have her again. And he refused to lose control twice in the same damn day.

The hell of it was, rather than being satisfied by their encounter, he had been wound even tighter than he was before. It was as if the tension, once released, had instantly coiled inside him again. There was no relief. Only more hunger. That one climax with Colleen had taken him to a place he hadn't even guessed existed—and his instincts wanted to go back.

Always before, bedding a woman who'd gotten under his skin had eased that itch. That nagging pulse of desire.

But with Colleen, it was just the opposite. He wanted her even more, now that he knew what having her was like.

Of course, after practically dumping her in her room and leaving her to fend for herself last night, there wasn't much chance of having more of her. He'd seen that look of surprise on her face when he'd walked away. Surprise, mixed with something else. Hurt? Maybe. Hell, didn't she understand he'd left her alone for her own good? Probably not.

Everything about Colleen was different. Her openness. The innocent pleasure always shining in her eyes. Her smile. Her laugh. The way she consistently looked for the good in people—and didn't stop until she found it. He liked her, damn it, and that had *not* been a part of the plan.

Racked with guilt over that tense, awkward goodbye, he'd devoted several mind-numbing hours to paperwork and emails and going over new contracts his lawyers had sent on. He'd also looked into Jack Reed to see if there was any more information to be gathered—there hadn't been. There was bound to be trouble if Reed was interested in Lassiter Media and Sage just added that complication to the growing list in his mind.

He'd buried himself so completely in the mundane tasks of maintaining the empire he was creating, it was long after midnight before he finally closed his books and trudged upstairs to his bedroom suite. Not that it had done him any good. How the hell could he sleep, knowing she was just down the hall?

No, instead of sleeping, he'd spent all night long reliving those moments with her in the cabin. When he did close his eyes, even briefly, her face was there. In front of him. And even if he *had* been able to sleep, she would have been in his dreams. The scent of her, the warmth of her. The slick slide of her legs around his hips.

By dawn, he'd given up on any pretense of rest and gone to work. God knew there was enough to do on a working ranch to exhaust him enough that even thoughts of sex with Colleen wouldn't be able to keep him awake.

"Pitiful. Seriously pitiful." Disgusted with himself, Sage tossed the hammer and nails into the bucket at his side, then sat back on his heels and stared up at the late-morning sky. The view from the roof of the main stable was pretty damn impressive, yet all he could think about was her.

He could see her, lying beneath him, staring up at him from the floor in a dusty cabin. *Nice seduction moves, Sage.* Pull out all the romantic stops to get her to spill her secrets. Way to go. Of course, his mind argued, he hadn't been thinking of seduction. Only the need to claim her. To be a part of her.

And now he wanted to do it all again.

He shifted his gaze from the sky to the ranch yard. He saw the place he'd built, the men who worked for him, his dog—a big golden retriever—taking a nap in the shade. The sky was that deep, startling blue you only found in the mountains. Thick white clouds sailed in the wind that shook the trees and rattled their leaves. In the corral, two of the cowboys were working with a yearling mare, putting her through her paces.

Sage smiled, grateful for the distraction from his own thoughts. That mare was going to be a star one day. She was already faster than most of the horses in his stable and she was proud enough that she liked winning.

Still smiling, he started down the ladder propped against the side of the stable, thankful that he hadn't fallen off the roof and broken his neck due to lack of concentration. Colleen had affected him so much that she'd ruined his focus, and yet he couldn't seem to mind.

Shaking his head, he neared the bottom of the ladder and dropped the bucket holding shingles, a hammer and nails to the ground.

"What were you doing up there?"

He went completely still, amazed at the sensation of heat that snaked through him just at the sound of her voice. He could hardly believe she'd stayed after what had happened yesterday. But he was glad she had. What the hell was wrong with him? A few weeks ago at the rehearsal dinner, he'd been intrigued enough by the look of her that he'd wanted to talk. Maybe take a quick roll in the hay if she was interested.

Now he knew her. He understood that there wasn't a dishonest bone in her body. Hell, there was just no way Colleen would even think of tricking or deceiving a sick old man. She hadn't slicked her way into a fortune. Hadn't cheated the Lassiter family. He knew that now. Knew her mind, her sense of humor, her generosity, and he knew what touching her did to him. She was paving right over all the roadblocks he'd had set up around his mind and heart for years...and it was damned disconcerting.

Colleen stood not a foot from the ladder, watching him, and he wondered why he hadn't heard her walk up. Too busy thinking of her, he told himself wryly. Yeah, this seduction plan was working out nicely.

"Loose shingles on the stable roof," he said, hitting the ground, then bending over to snatch up the bucket before straightening to look into her eyes. Instantly, he felt that punch of something raw and elemental—and it was getting harder to ignore.

He'd missed her at breakfast, too. Deliberately. He'd grabbed a cup of coffee and one of his housekeeper's famous muffins and headed outside—where he'd stayed, keeping as busy as he could. "The wind kicked up last night, and after last winter a few of the shingles were ready to go."

She looked up, squinting into the late-morning sunlight, as if she could see where he'd been working. "You do the repairs yourself?"

"Sometimes," he admitted, and hefted the ladder across one shoulder. When he started walking toward the equipment shed where tools were stored, she followed him. "Why sound so surprised? It is my ranch."

The golden retriever rose lazily from his spot by the barn and stretched before trotting to Colleen's side. She stopped, dropped to one knee and smoothed both hands across the top of the lucky dog's head. A hell of a thing, Sage thought, when a man envied his dog.

"He's so sweet," she said, throwing a quick look up at Sage. "But I don't understand his name."

In spite of what he was feeling, Sage choked out a laugh. "You mean Beback?"

She scrubbed the dog's ears, then stood up, tucking her hands into the pockets of her jeans. "Yes. What kind of name is that?"

Shrugging, Sage said, "When he was a pup, he kept running off into the forest, but he was always running right back. One of the guys said it reminded him of a famous line in a movie...*I'll be back.*"

Colleen laughed and, God, he loved the sound of it. And as soon as that thought slid through his mind, he pushed it back out again. *Love?* What the hell?

"Beback. I like it," she said with a grin as she watched the dog race off after one of the cowboys. "I always wanted a dog. In fact, I'm going to get one as soon as I find my place."

"Not the Jackson cabin?"

She threw him a quick look and her eyes flared as if she were remembering their encounter. "I don't know yet. Maybe."

Nodding, Sage continued on to the shed and sensed rather than heard her follow him. And naturally, she was still talking.

"Going back to me being surprised at you doing the repairs to one of the buildings…I don't know, I guess I thought you would have one of the men who work for you do the minor repairs." She waved one hand to encompass the whole of the yard and the half dozen or so ranch hands working at different tasks.

His long strides never slowed, though he knew she had to be hurrying to keep up with him. "J.D. always said, 'Don't be afraid to do your own work. Men will respect you for it.'"

Frowning, he wondered where that had come from. He wasn't really in the habit of quoting his father. Yet it seemed that since J.D. died, Sage had thought more about him than he had in years. And the situation wasn't helped by Colleen's presence. After all, the only reason they were together at all was because of the old man.

"So you do have some good memories of J.D."

"Didn't say they were good ones," he muttered, leading the way into the shed. "Just memories."

Inside it was cool and dark. The walls were covered with hooks from which clean, cared-for tools hung neatly. One wall contained a long workbench with drawers beneath it and the rest of the place held everything from shovels to snowplows.

With her standing so close to him, it was hard to keep hold of his own self-control. Desire pulsed heavily inside him even while his brain kept shouting for caution. If he had any hope of keeping his mind clear, he needed some distance between them. Releasing a breath, Colleen glanced around the shed. "I won't need anywhere near this much equipment," she said as if to herself.

"You'll need plenty of it, though," he warned, taking the opportunity to spread a little more doubt in her mind. "Snowblower or plow. Shovels, pickaxes, and by the way, that old Jeep of yours isn't going to cut it up here, either."

"What?" She flashed him a stunned look. "Why not?"

"For one thing, it's too small. You'll need a truck."

At that, she laughed a little. "Why would I need a truck? My Jeep has been fine for me in the snow."

"The wheelbase is too short," he told her, and shook his head when he saw the blank confusion in her eyes. "Too easily tipped over. And in a high wind on the mountain road…"

She shivered as he'd meant her to—because the thought of her navigating those switchback curves alone in a storm gave him a damn heart attack.

"For another thing," he added, "you'll need the truck bed, because there's no trash collection here. You'll have to make trips to the dump yourself."

She chewed at her bottom lip and Sage felt a confusing mix of satisfaction and guilt. He didn't necessarily want to be the one to ruin her dream. But hell if he wanted her alone in a situation she wasn't prepared for either.

"Where's the dump?"

"I can show you." And that would serve as a negative, too. Once she got a whiff of the dump, she'd be less inclined to have to go there regularly.

"Okay…"

"There's no mail delivery up here either," he said

while he still held her attention. "You'll have to get a P.O. box in town."

She sighed. "I hadn't thought it would be so complicated." Turning in a slow circle, she let her gaze wander over the walls of tools as if she were trying to figure out how to use them. "All I want to do is live on the mountain, closer to where my patients will be."

"Most things generally are complicated," he said, emptying the work bucket he'd brought in with him. He opened drawers, returning the hammer, nails and left-over shingles to their proper places and when he was finished, he turned to find Colleen staring at him, a smile as bright as sunlight on her face. "And when you live up here—especially alone—you have to expect to take care of a lot of things most people don't worry about… what are you smiling at?"

"You." She shrugged. "It's funny, but I don't think I ever pictured you as being a fix-it kind of guy."

"Yeah, well." He closed the drawer and walked to set the bucket down in a corner of the shed. "J.D. had Dylan and I working all over Big Blue when we were kids. The two of us had a chores list that would make a grown man weep. We worked with the cattle and the horses, learned how to rebuild engines and shingle roofs when they needed it." He leaned one hip against the workbench, folded his arms across his chest and continued, "J.D. thought we should know the place from the ground up. Be familiar with everything so we were never at the mercy of anyone else. During school, we had plenty of time for homework, but during summer, he worked us both."

She tipped her head to one side and looked up at him. "Sounds like it was hard work."

"It was," he admitted, realizing he hadn't thought about those times in years. When they were kids, he and Dylan had hated all the chores. But they'd learned. Not that Dylan needed most of those lessons today, what with spearheading the Lassiter Grill Group. But Sage could admit, at least to himself, that everything he'd learned on the Big Blue had helped him run his own ranch better than he might have done otherwise. Sourly, he acknowledged that growing up as J.D. Lassiter's son had prepared him for the kind of life he had always wanted to live.

All those hot summers spent training horses, riding the range rounding up stray cattle. The long hours sweeping out the stable and the barn. The backbreaking task of clearing brush away from the main house. He and his younger brother had become part of the crew working Big Blue. The other wranglers and cowboys accepted them as equals, not the boss's adopted kids.

Shaking his head, Sage looked back on it all now and could see that J.D. had been helping them build their own places on Big Blue. To feel a part of the ranch. He'd been giving them a foundation. Roots to replace the ones they'd lost.

"Crafty old goat," he muttered, with just a touch of admiration for the father he had resented for so long.

"He really was, wasn't he?"

Sage caught the indulgent smile on her face and stiffened. But Colleen was unaware of the change in him, because she kept talking.

"He used to make me laugh," she was saying. "He couldn't get out much in his last couple of months, but he managed to steer everyone around him into doing just what he wanted them to do. He ran the ranch from his bed and his recliner. He even convinced me to accompany him to the rehearsal dinner," she added softly, "when I *knew* he wasn't well enough for the stress of the evening."

"That wasn't your fault," he said quickly.

"Wasn't it?" Her gaze locked with his. "I was his nurse. Supposed to guard his failing health, not give in to him when I knew it was dangerous." She reached up and pushed her hair back from her face, and suddenly Sage thought of how it had felt to have his own hands in that thick, silky mass.

Gritting his teeth, he pushed that thought aside and only said, "J.D. had a way of getting just what he wanted from folks. You shouldn't feel guilty about being one of them."

"He was a lovely man," she whispered. "Hard, but fair. Tough, but he loved his family. All of you. He talked about you all so much…"

Sage's ears perked up. "Did he?"

"Oh, yes." She walked closer to him, running her fingertips along the edge of the workbench. "He was so proud of Dylan's work with the grill. And he talked about Angie all the time—"

She broke off, as if remembering that J.D.'s will sort of belied that last statement.

"And you." She moved even closer and he caught her scent on the still, cool air. The scent that had haunted him all night long. Her eyes shone up at him with innocence and pleasure, as if she was really enjoying being able to share all of this with him. "He took so much pride in what you've built. He used to go on and on about how you made your first million while you were in school, and how he'd had to go to great lengths to convince you to stay at college when all you really wanted to do was build your own ranch—"

Sage's vision went red. And just like that, the seductive, sensual air between him and Colleen sizzled into an inferno that apparently only he could sense. His mind burned and thoughts chased each other through the darkness spreading through him. Years-old fury reawakened as if it had never gone to sleep, and he trembled with the force of the control required to keep from shouting out his rage.

Her voice was just a buzz of sound now, but even through the anger churning within, he could see that Colleen clearly believed that she'd scored a point. That she'd made Sage see his father as the *caring, thoughtful, generous* man she thought he was. That she'd found a way past the old angers and hurts. But instead, all she had done was relight the fuse that had been smoldering for years.

He took a breath and interrupted her stream of conversation. "Yeah. He was proud. Too damn proud. And he wasn't the kindhearted, feeble old gentleman you think you knew."

"What are you talking about?"

He threw a glance at the open shed door and the ranch yard beyond. Golden sunlight washed over his ranch, making the inside of the shed seem even darker in comparison. But damned if he'd have this talk out in public so that anyone could overhear. He strode across the straw-littered floor, slammed the door and threw the lock. Only then did he turn around to face Colleen again, and in the back of his mind, he noted that her eyes were wary.

"You met J.D. when he was old and tired and looking to find the fast track into heaven," Sage finally said and had the small satisfaction of seeing her blink in surprise. "I knew him back in the day and trust me, he wasn't a sweetheart. He was domineering, a know-it-all and damned arrogant with it."

One dark blond eyebrow lifted. "Remind you of anyone?"

He snorted in spite of the anger bubbling into an ugly brew in the pit of his stomach. "Okay, I can accept that maybe I picked up a few of his less pleasant traits along the way. But I never—" Damn. The words were stuck in his throat like bitter bile. He hadn't talked about this in years. And he'd *never* told anyone else about this. Not Dylan. Not Angie. The only person he had ever been open with about it was J.D. Because the old man himself was at the heart of it.

Shaking his head fiercely, as if he could dislodge the blackness wrapped around his memories, he muttered, "You said he wanted me to stay in college. That he told you he *talked* me into it."

"That's what he said, yes."

"Well, then, he had a really selective memory," Sage said flatly. "Because he didn't talk me into anything. He maneuvered me until he got his way. Just like he did everything else in his life."

"What do you mean, maneuvered?"

He hadn't meant to allow old memories to nearly choke him as they rushed up from the black bottom of his heart to spill through his mind like tar. But there they were, and he'd come too far to stop now.

"Unlike J.D., I never figured that I knew best how another man should live his life. I never made it my business to take something from a person just because I could."

"*What* are you talking about?"

"I was in college. My sophomore year. Twenty years old and I figured I had all the answers." He pushed one hand through his hair and tipped his head back to look up through the skylight at the cloud-scudded sky. Even with his age-old fury pushing his words, they caught in his throat and had to be forced out. But if he was going to say it, he was going to look into those oh-so-innocent eyes that saw only the good in people. That way he could be a witness when she finally had to admit that J.D. was nothing like she'd thought he was.

"What happened?" The concern in her voice was as real as the touch of her hand on his arm. The electrical whip of heat that sliced through him did battle with the anger and lost.

He snorted. "What happened? J.D. happened. I went home one night and told him that I was leaving school."

"Why?"

His gaze speared into hers. "I was in love. Or at least I thought I was. I told J.D. we were going to get married and start up my ranch."

Her voice was soft and uncertain as she asked, "What did he say?"

"Oh," Sage said on a sharp bark of laughter, "J.D. said all the right things. Told me he'd help me get into the inheritance my parents left me. Wasn't much," he added, "but it would've given me a start."

"That's good though, isn't it?" Her eyes were shimmering with hurt and he didn't know if it was for him or herself. "J.D. said he'd help you."

"Yeah, and then the next day, when I got to my girlfriend's place, her roommate told me she was gone and wouldn't be back." Amazing, Sage thought, that it could still hurt after all these years. That the betrayal was as sharp. The fury as thick.

"Why would she leave?"

He looked at her and quirked one eyebrow, inviting her to fill in the blanks. When she didn't, he did it for her. "She left me a note. Told me that it had been fun, but she was moving to Paris to paint. And she wasn't supposed to let me in on it, but apparently she didn't mind turning on J.D., either, because she told me in the note that he'd paid her two hundred thousand bucks to leave."

Colleen looked up at him, and for the first time in her life, didn't have the slightest clue what to say. This J.D. was not the man she had known. How could he have hurt his son so badly? And while her heart hurt for Sage, there was pain for herself, as well.

Sage had been in love. He'd wanted to get married. And though it was years ago, a part of her ached hearing the words.

He scrubbed both hands across his face. "I called him on it right away and he was furious that Megan had told me what he'd done." He shook his head and choked out another laugh. "He didn't see anything wrong with what he'd done, of course, but he was pissed as hell that I'd found out about it. Told me he'd done it for my sake. That Megan wasn't the kind of woman to stand by a man—"

She opened her mouth and he spoke quickly to cut her off.

"—before you can say it, yeah, he was right about Megan. If she had loved me, she never would have taken the money. But he should have let *me* find out the truth about her myself. Instead, he charged in, just like always, and rearranged the world to suit himself."

Megan was a fool. An idiot. She'd had this proud, strong, yes, *arrogant* man's love and she'd sold it. Colleen would never have betrayed him. She would have been proud to have his love, to work with him to build a ranch, a legacy for the family they would build and—

Colleen's throat closed up. All of a sudden she couldn't breathe. Couldn't stop the sting of tears in her eyes. What on earth was wrong with…

Oh, God. *She was in love.*

For the first time in her life, she was madly, completely, passionately in love with a man who probably would never return the feeling. The realization staggered her and if she hadn't had the workbench behind her as a brace, she might have just slumped to the floor. How was she going to get past this feeling? How could she possibly be in love with a man who wanted nothing to do with love and family? Who believed that love meant betrayal?

Sage was still talking and she forced herself to listen. He didn't need to know what she was feeling, that her heart was breaking. What he needed was to get past the old pain still gnawing on him. "Sage…"

"Forget it. You can't say anything, Colleen. J.D. was a bastard. End of story."

Her own feelings didn't matter right now, she told herself. What *did* matter was the pain Sage was still in. She couldn't bear seeing him cling to old injuries that were only hurting him, keeping him from moving on, and understanding that though his father had treated him badly, it wasn't because he hadn't loved him.

Colleen moved in closer, laid one hand on his chest

and said, "What he did was terrible, you're right. But he did it because he loved you."

"Hell of a way to prove it," he muttered. "He betrayed me, bottom line. And so did Megan, though in the long run, she did me a favor."

"Can't you say J.D. did, too?"

He snorted. "Don't know that I'm ready to thank him. But looking back, I can see that I mistook lust for love and I'm guessing J.D. saw that more clearly than I did back then." He blew out a breath and Colleen saw the anger fade from his eyes as he began to let go of the past. "I can say that if he hadn't stuck his nose in, I might not be standing here in front of a woman who turns my blood to fire with a look."

Instantly, Colleen's whole body lit up as if a sudden fever erupted inside her. She loved him. She wanted him. She stared into his eyes and knew that though he might not love her back, his desire was real and every bit as powerful as her own. "Sage…"

"I'm done talking about J.D. right now, Colleen," he murmured, dropping both hands to the workbench on either side of her, pinning her in place. "I've been trying to stay away from you—"

"I know," she said. "Why?"

"Because I want you too much. You're all I think about. All I give a flying damn about. You're in my blood, Colleen."

"You're in mine, too," she whispered, reaching up to cup his face between her palms. Her thumbs traced across his cheekbones and he held perfectly still as she went up on her toes, moved in and kissed him.

That soft brush of her lips against his was a benediction of sorts. A wiping away of the past and a welcome into the present—the future?

He fell into her kiss willingly, eagerly, and wrapped his arms around her. Colleen gave herself up to the moment, letting go of everything but the magic shimmering in the air between them.

But just as the kiss was deepening, spiraling out of control, Sage pulled back, looked down at her and muttered, "Damned if we're going to be together in an old cabin and then in an equipment shed where any one of my cowboys could glance in the window for a peek."

She flushed and laughed, burying her face briefly against his chest. "I forgot entirely where we were."

"Yeah, you have that effect on me, too," he confessed. "But today we're going to try an actual *bed*. Come with me."

He took her hand and led her out of the shed toward the main house and all Colleen could think was, she would go with him anywhere.

Ten

She woke up early in the master bedroom to find that Sage was already up and gone.

Colleen sighed and stretched languorously in the big bed she'd shared with him all night. Her mind filled with images of the night before and bubbles of residual heat slid through her bloodstream like champagne. She'd only managed about two hours' sleep all night, but she'd never felt more awake, more aware.

Who would have guessed that *love* could heighten every sense? Could make you both grateful and miserable with the kind of feelings that were so overwhelming? She couldn't stay, she knew she couldn't. She loved him and he didn't love her and never the twain would meet just like when it happened in those literary, depressing love stories.

But God, she didn't want to go. Her gaze fixed on

the wall of windows and French doors leading to a wood deck, beyond which she saw an amazing sweep of stormy sky that was punctuated by the tips of pine trees. It looked as though they would get another storm, and she knew she should go before that storm hit. Now all she needed was the courage to make the move. She was in love, but he wasn't. In fact, he would probably panic and run if he knew how she felt about him. But when she remembered the tenderness, the amazing heat that spiraled between them when they made love, it was hard not to dream that one day, he might love her back.

"Oh, God," she murmured, pulling her pillow out from under her head to drop it onto her face. "Try not to be a complete idiot, Colleen. Sex isn't love. Just because he's good at it doesn't mean he cares. He's just… thorough."

She threw one arm across that pillow so that her voice was muffled and she wouldn't have to listen to herself. Honestly, this was a serious mess. Falling in love was just—unavoidable, she thought. Now she had to work out what to do about it. Keep her mouth shut, obviously. And get off this mountain as quickly as possible. Because the longer she stayed, the harder it would be to eventually walk away.

Just as that depressing thought took up root in her mind, Colleen's cell phone rang and she rolled out of bed to grab her jeans off the floor. Fumbling through the pockets, she found her phone, saw the caller ID and winced. "Hi, Mom."

"Hi, sweetie, how's it going?"

"Great, really. Um…" She looked around for *something* to slip on. She couldn't just stand there naked and chat with her mother. Finally settling for a sheet, she snaked it off the bed and wrapped it around her.

"So." Laura's voice was bright and happy. "Did you find the house you want to buy?"

Memories of the cabin rose up in her mind and she smiled wistfully. "I think so," she said, "but I'm still looking."

Because she loved that cabin and thought it would be perfect for her. But the question was, would she be able to live with the memories of what she and Sage had done there once they weren't together anymore? Could she really face those memories every day?

"That's wonderful, honey. It's so nice of Sage to take the time to show you around."

"Yep, very nice." And so much more.

"I know it's early to call, but I had to tell you, your aunt Donna is coming for a visit next week."

"That's great." She could hear the excitement in her mother's voice and Colleen sent another silent thank-you to J.D. for making this possible. Even if her own life was teetering on the brink of despair, at least her mother was having fun.

"We're going to plan our trip together and get our passport photos taken together," Laura said in a tangled rush of words. She kept talking, outlining her plans and laughing more than Colleen had heard her laugh in years. Finally, though, her mom slowed down and said, "You're awfully quiet."

"What?" Damn. She should have been paying closer attention. Her mother always had been really good at picking up on Colleen's moods.

"Never mind trying to play it cool, kiddo. Spill it."

Colleen dropped onto the edge of the bed, stared out

at the view and took a deep breath before saying, "I screwed up."

"Impossible."

She laughed and a little of her depression lifted. "Thanks, Mom."

"Tell me what's wrong, sweetie."

"I'm in love with a man who likes me."

"But that's wonderful." Laura practically cheered.

Colleen shook her head and with one hand, pushed her hair back from her face. "I think you missed the most important part in that last sentence, Mom. He *likes* me. He doesn't love me."

"He will, though. How could he not?"

God bless mothers, Colleen thought with a sad smile. Though her mom would always support her, always believe in her, there was no way she could understand how Colleen was feeling right now. Her parents had fallen in love at first sight. They'd only known each other a month before they got married and they'd stayed deeply in love until the day Colleen's father died. So with that kind of background, her mother would never be able to see just how hopeless Colleen's situation was.

"It's not that easy." Not when his past held memories of a woman who had betrayed him.

"Who said it was supposed to be easy?" her mother asked, then added, "Okay, yes, your dad and I had it easy. We found each other and it all fell together. But Sage likes you. That's not so far from love."

Outside, the sky opened up and rain pelted the windows. They'd had sun, snow and now rain in just a few days. Colleen shivered a little and wondered if the storm was an omen. Then she dismissed that thought. No need to get crazy here.

"Have you told him how you feel?"

"Of course not," she said, horrified at the thought. She'd like to hang on to a little bit of dignity if she could. "I can't admit to that. How humiliating."

"Or," her mother said slyly, "how liberating. You risk nothing but a little pride. And honey, love is worth any price you have to pay."

A few minutes later she hung up, but her mother's words were still echoing through Colleen's mind. Was she right? Should she tell Sage what she was feeling? Or should she just pack up her heart before it got bruised and run back to reality?

An hour later, she was dressed and downstairs, looking for a cup of coffee. She was packed and would be leaving as soon as she spoke to Sage. She just still hadn't made up her mind what exactly to say to him and was hoping caffeine would help her think more clearly. When she heard Sage's voice, she followed the sound without even thinking about it. Walking down the long, gloomy hall, her sneakered footsteps were quiet on the wood floor. She tapped gently on his office door, then opened it.

He was sitting at his desk, holding the phone to his ear, which explained her hearing his voice. His back was to her, his gaze fixed on the raging storm beyond the wide glass window. Adrenaline pulsed through her as he started speaking again, as if her body was tuned to the timbre and richness of his voice. But before she could back out of the room and give him privacy for his call, *what* he was saying caught her attention.

"Dylan," he said, sounding bored and impatient as he talked to his brother, "dating Colleen was the only sure way to find out exactly what J.D. was up to before he died."

Her heart stopped and a thin sliver of air worked its way down her lungs. Blindly, she reached out one hand to the doorjamb and held on as if it meant her life.

"She was the closest to the old man and it's entirely possible that she knows something she's not even aware of," Sage continued.

Colleen felt sick. Her heartbeat was slow. Heavy. Like a movie played in extremely slow motion. Ice dropped into the pit of her churning stomach and the cold seemed to spread, snaking out tentacles that reached throughout her body until she shivered with reaction.

She should leave.

She knew she should turn and run. Hit the front door, race to her car and get off the mountain. But she couldn't move. It was as if her feet were nailed to the floor. She wanted to be struck deaf so she wouldn't have to hear any more. She wanted to have never come downstairs. To have never come here to this ranch at all.

Sage shook his head and laughed at whatever his brother was saying. "You're wrong, Dylan. Trust me, I'm not getting too close to Colleen. I don't *do* close. Besides, this isn't about what I *want*—it's about what I want to find out."

Did she make a sound? She might have. A tiny gasp. A small moan. Of course she did. How could her body contain so much pain without letting some of it escape? Whatever that sound was, he heard it, because he slowly swiveled around in his chair, spotted her across the room and said simply, "Colleen."

Funny. It was the look in his eyes that finally freed her enough to run. The shock. The surprise. The *guilt*. By the time he slammed the phone into its cradle, she was gone.

* * *

Panic roared into life in Sage's chest and had him bolting from his office, racing after her, determined to catch her. To explain. To— Hell. He didn't know what he'd do.

"Damn it, Colleen, *wait!*" He caught her at the front door and slammed one hand on the heavy oak panel so she couldn't yank it open no matter how hard she tried.

"Get away," she said and he heard tears choking her voice.

Pain lanced him as he called himself all kinds of vicious but accurate names.

"I mean it, Sage," she muttered thickly. "Let me go."

"It's raining, Colleen. You can't leave in a storm."

"I know how to drive in the rain—and I'm leaving."

"I can't let you do that." That panic was still bubbling up inside him and staring down into her damp eyes, it only got worse. She was trying to leave and he couldn't let her. Not like this.

"What you heard back there? It wasn't true." He hung his head and gave it a shake before finding the strength to meet those tear-filled blue eyes again. "I was just trying to get Dylan off my back, that's all."

"No," she said, her mouth twisting as if she were trying desperately to keep her bottom lip from quivering. "It was true. All of it. I'm only surprised I didn't see it sooner."

Seeing tears clouding her clear, beautiful eyes tore at him. Knowing he had caused it nearly killed him. The worst kind of bastard, he'd hurt a woman who didn't deserve it, all to cover his own ass and save his pride with his brother.

"Why else would you ever go for a woman like me?"

Shaking her head, she lifted her chin and he saw what that defiant, proud move cost her. "So don't tell me that conversation with your brother wasn't true. Recent behavior notwithstanding, I'm not an idiot, Sage. Now open this door and let me leave."

"You don't really want to go and I don't want you to," he said, gaze moving over her lovely features, searing her face into his mind. He drew her scent in deep and felt her permeate every cell in his body.

He should have locked the damn office door. Then this wouldn't be an issue. She never would have overheard him. They could have gone on as they were, and both of them would have been happy. Instead, he had to try to unravel the damage he'd done.

The thing was, he hadn't meant a damn thing he'd said to his brother. He just hadn't wanted to admit to himself, let alone Dylan, that he'd come to…care for Colleen. Oh, it might have started out differently, using her as a means to an end, but somewhere along the line, that had changed. Into what, he couldn't say. All he was sure of was that he hated seeing her in pain. Hated knowing he was the cause.

Bending his head, he kissed her and refused to allow her to turn her face from his. Wouldn't let her ignore the fire between them. And in seconds, in spite of the turmoil churning inside her, she was kissing him back. His heart gave one wild lurch as he realized that maybe, just maybe, he could still salvage what he had with her. He wrapped his arms around her and held her tightly, losing himself, as always, in the heat that engulfed him the moment they came together.

Seconds, minutes, it could have been hours that passed as they stood, wrapped up in each other, mouths fused, hearts beating in tandem. But when he tried to draw back, to lead her toward the stairs and his bedroom, Colleen said, "No."

He stared at her, confused by the refusal. "What?"

"No," she said again, pulling away from him, taking a step back to increase the space between them. "I won't go back upstairs with you, Sage. I can't."

He shoved one hand through his hair. "But you kissed me back just now. You believed me when I told you that I didn't mean any of what you heard."

"Didn't you?" Her eyes were wounded. There was no sign of tears now, but the cool detachment he saw in her expression worried Sage more than a flood of tears might have. "Why did you first come to see me, Sage? Why did you first want to spend time with me?"

Instead of answering, he asked a question of his own. "Why are you doing this?"

She laughed shortly, but the sound was harsh and strained. "I really don't want to, but I have no choice. So tell me why, Sage."

He wouldn't lie to her. Couldn't bring himself to look into those honest, oh-so-innocent eyes and lie just to save his own ass. He'd bring her more pain and it would rip him apart, but she deserved the damned truth.

"You know why." As his gaze locked with hers, he saw her eyes widen slightly and another slash of pain dart across their surfaces.

"So it's true."

"It's not true *now*," he countered and took a step toward her. He stopped when she backed away, maintaining the distance between them. "I didn't know you," he said, forcing himself to keep meeting her eyes, acknowledging the pain he was causing her even as it sliced at him, too. "All I knew was that J.D.'s will had been changed. He'd cheated my sister out of what should have been hers, and J.D.'s private nurse was suddenly a millionaire."

She sucked in a gulp of air and the gasping sound filled the quiet house. "You really believed I had somehow tricked J.D. into leaving me money and cheating your sister?"

"Don't you get it, Colleen? *Nothing* was making sense. J.D. turned on his daughter. Thinking you were somehow behind it all made as much sense as anything else." It sounded so stupid now, knowing her as he did. But in his own defense, hadn't he had his own experience with J.D. paying women off? "Can you blame me? You know what my father did to me once before. He betrayed me then…and now, from the damn *grave,* he's doing the same thing to Angie."

She shook her head sadly. "You've let that one horrible experience color your whole life, haven't you?"

"Why shouldn't I? It was a valuable lesson and I learned it well."

Her luscious mouth twisted into a parody of a smile that was almost harder to see than the single tear escaping her eye to roll along her cheek.

"Oh, Sage," she said, her voice aching with the hurt he'd just dealt her. "What you *didn't* learn was that J.D. didn't do that to hurt you. He did it to protect you. That's what we do for people we love."

"*Protect* me?" He laughed, astonished that she could still take J.D.'s side in this, in spite of everything. "How? By making me doubt myself, my judgment? By ensuring that I wouldn't trust another damn soul? Some help."

Shaking her head again, she looked at him with disappointment. "You chose that path, Sage. Your father didn't put you on it." Her voice was so quiet he had to strain to hear it over the thundering beat of his own heart. "He was trying to save you from more pain later on down the road." She paused, then hurried on before he could speak. "Sure, he made mistakes. But people do. Especially the people who love us."

What the hell was he supposed to do with a woman like her? She continually looked for the good in people—and had found it in J.D. Despite what he'd done to Sage so many years ago, the old man had done the best he could by *all* of his children, and maybe Sage was now willing to accept that. If he did, it just made the will that much more perplexing.

As confusing as the woman standing before him. He didn't want to examine those feelings. Didn't want to explore the wild explosion of thoughts and sensations churning in his mind. All he wanted was *her*.

And he couldn't have her.

A tight fist was squeezing his heart and lungs, making it almost impossible to draw an easy breath. Finally though, he said, "So can't you see that I made a mistake? About you? Can't you forgive that and let it go?"

That sad smile curved her mouth again as she murmured, "I can forgive it, but I'm still leaving."

"Why?" That one word was a demand.

"Because I love you, Sage," she said simply. "And I deserve better."

Staggered, he couldn't think of a single thing to say. She loved him? She *loved* him. And she was leaving anyway? She was opening the front door and the sound and scent of a driving rain sneaked across the threshold. She loved him. Those three words kept echoing in his mind, rattling his soul.

"Before I go, though, there is one thing J.D. told me that you should know."

His eyes narrowed on her as suspicion leaped up to the base of his throat. "What?"

"God. Even now you're still wondering if I betrayed you or not."

"No." He denied it. He knew she wasn't capable of betrayal. Knew that she was too intrinsically honest to be a part of any deception. Just as he knew that when she said she loved him, she meant every word.

"J.D. was proud of you. And he regretted that the two of you weren't close." She blew out a breath. "He was heartsick that his sons believed he didn't care."

He wished he could believe that she was lying about all of this. Because if it was all true, then he and J.D. had both been cheated of the relationship they might have had.

"He also told me," she said softly, "that he left you the Lassiter Media shares so that you would always remember that you're family. So you would realize that family is important and that *love* is all that matters."

Then she was gone.

And he was alone.

Two weeks crawled past.

Sage didn't see her. Didn't speak to her. Didn't do much of anything, really. In that first week, he couldn't give a damn about the ranch that had once been the most important thing in his life. He didn't care about stock prices or the phone calls and emails he kept getting from the various boards of the companies he sat on.

All he could think about was Colleen and the last words she'd said to him. Words that J.D. had often said when Sage was a kid. *Family. Love was everything.*
Love.

Sage hadn't really known what that was until Colleen had loved him and left him. As a younger man, he'd mistaken lust for love and just as Colleen said, he'd allowed that one poor choice to color the rest of his life. He'd cut himself off, in theory to protect himself, but in reality all he'd been doing was hiding.

Well, he was through hiding. That's why he spent the second week setting wheels in motion. There were things to do. Things to be said. A life to be lived.

When Sage walked through the front door of Big Blue, he looked around and for the first time in years, he didn't cringe from the memories rushing toward him. His heart was still heavy, but that had nothing to do with J.D. Not anymore. Sage had finally come to accept that his father was just a man, as capable of making mistakes as anyone. God knew Sage had made plenty. Especially lately.

"Sage! What're you doing here?" Angie came down the stairs, a smile on her face, and rushed toward her oldest brother for a hug. "I'm so glad to see you. And hey, *honored* that you left your ranch."

"Yeah, well," he told her, "a lot of things have changed." And how was she going to take what he had to say to her? He didn't want to hurt his sister. Hell, he'd do anything to avoid that. He just didn't see a way around it.

"No kidding," she said wryly and he knew that she was still thinking about the will and what J.D. had done to her.

It was the perfect opening for what he'd come to say. They had talked about this before, but at the time, he hadn't made the final decision that he now had to share with his sister.

"Angie, we can't fight the will."

"What?" Confused, she said, "Why not?"

He took both of her hands in his, glanced around the entry hall and felt the years of being a Lassiter settle down onto his shoulders. He was J.D.'s son and it was high time he started acting like it.

"Because if we do that and lose, a lot of people could be hurt. Marlene. Chance…" *Colleen,* he thought but didn't say.

"But you said we'd do something about this. That we'd figure it all out. I thought you were on *my* side."

His heart squeezed. "I am on your side, honey. You're my sister and I love you. But you know, too—hell, we *all* know, that J.D. loved you to death." He squeezed her hands. "So he had a reason for what he did no matter how crazy it seems to us. We're going to sit back and trust that our father did the right thing."

"That's easy for you to say." Angie yanked her hands from his and glared at him. "Dad didn't turn on you."

"Yeah, I know. Just like I know that J.D. had a *reason* for everything he ever did. We just have to find out the reason behind this."

"And that'll make it better?" The short laugh that shot from her throat told him how she felt about that.

"Didn't say that." Shaking his head, Sage looked at his sister and tried not to see the unshed tears glittering in her eyes. "We both know J.D. would never do anything to deliberately hurt you, so there's a reason for what he did. We're going to trust it's a good one."

"I can't believe this." There was hurt in her eyes, but mostly she was furious.

Well, he could deal with an angry sister. Anger he understood.

"Angie, I spent a lot of years mad at J.D. I wasted what I could have had." Disgusted with himself and sad that missed chances could never be recaptured, he said, "I'm through wasting time. I'm through holding a grudge against our father. I love you, Angie, but I won't support you if you try to fight the will."

"Sage—"

"You, me, Dylan," he said, cutting off whatever she might have said, "we're family. And love is all that matters."

She choked out a strained laugh. "You sound just like Dad."

Sage grinned. "About time, don't you think?"

Colleen hadn't expected love.

At thirty-one, she'd long ago given up on the whole Prince Charming thing and had made up her mind to enjoy her career and her life, and if love found her, then great. If not, that would be okay, too.

Well, love had found her. When she'd least expected it, love had arrived. "And lucky me, now I know exactly what it's like to try to live without it."

The past two weeks had been awful. Just awful. She was tired of putting on a happy face for her mother—but it was necessary because she didn't want her mom worrying. And it was a strain pretending everything would be great to Jenna—who wanted to drive up the mountain and kick Sage. The worst part of it all was trying to get by on fifteen minutes of sleep every night.

Sage was on her mind all the time. She couldn't sleep, couldn't eat—at least she'd lost six pounds—and just the thought of never being with him again made Colleen want to crawl into a hole and die. How was it possible, she wondered, for your whole world to change completely in just a matter of weeks?

Looking back, she could see how it had all happened. She'd been half in love with Sage from the moment J.D. had told her the first story about his oldest son. She was lost from the moment she'd seen him at the rehearsal dinner. And now she was just lost.

Sitting at the table in her condo kitchen, she looked over the sales papers and signed her name at every highlighted X. The condo was sold and she was now officially homeless. She still had to finish qualifying as a nurse practitioner, but most of that could be done online. And when she had to come to Cheyenne for classes, she was willing to drive down off the mountain to do it. She was ready for change. Ready to start living the rest of her life.

All she needed now was to find a place to live.

"Poor little rich girl," she murmured, flipping through the pages. Three million dollars and no home to call her own. She'd have to start over, looking for a place, because she couldn't buy that cabin. Not now. Not ever. She wouldn't be able to live there, remembering the passion, the incredible sense of rightness that she'd felt with Sage so briefly.

"It's okay," she told herself, signing her name with a flourish. "I'll find something else. There's more than one cabin in the mountains. I'll still—"

God, who was she trying to kid? Who was she being brave for? She was all alone here. No mom. No Jenna.

She could cry and wail and weep if she wanted to—for all the good it would do her. It had already been two weeks. Sage had forgotten all about her and it would really be a good thing if she could do the same.

Nodding, she picked up the sheaf of papers, slid them back into the envelope her real estate agent had dropped off and then sealed it. It was done. Her house was sold. Her new life was about to begin. She only wished she could be happy about that.

When the doorbell rang, she jumped up, eager for any distraction to take her mind off her depressing thoughts. To keep her too busy to think of Sage and everything that might have been.

She pulled the door open and there he was. For a second, his presence didn't really compute. It was as if she'd spent so much time thinking about him that her mind had actually conjured a vision of him just for her. But that silly thought was gone the moment he opened his mouth.

"We have to talk."

"No, we don't." Colleen shook her head and tried to close the door, but his booted foot kept it open. "I'm really not a masochist, Sage, so if you don't mind I'd appreciate you just going away. If you're here to apologize, thanks. You're forgiven. Happy trails and all of that."

God, what it cost her to tell him no. But how could she let him back in, even temporarily? *Salt, meet wound.* No. She just couldn't do it. Already she wasn't sleeping or eating and her eyes were constantly red from all the tears. She had nothing left.

"I'm not here to apologize," he muttered through the gap between her door and the wall.

"You're *not?*" She glared at him through that same gap. "You should be."

"You already forgave me, remember?"

Frowning, she was forced to admit he had a point. "Fine. Then there's no reason for you to be here at all. So go away."

"Beback misses you."

"That's just mean," she snapped. He knew how much she liked his dog. How much she wanted one of her own.

"I miss you."

"You miss the sex," she countered because she simply would not let herself believe anything else. She was through building castles in the air. Just because he was here didn't mean anything between them had changed.

"Sure I do. Don't you?"

She looked into his eyes, those really amazing, wonderful, soulful eyes and couldn't deny it. Naturally she missed the sex. "Yes."

"And you miss me," he said softly.

Oh, she did. She really did.

"I'll get over it," she told him and shoved harder on the door. But the man was just too strong for her.

"I don't want you to get over it. Or me."

"Sage…" She sighed, leaned her forehead against the door and murmured, "*Please* go away?"

He reached through the gap, covered her hand with one of his, and Colleen felt that so familiar zing of heat that whispered inside her, urging her to listen. To let him in. To remember how good they were together. But remembering wouldn't change anything, so why go there?

"Why are you here?" She pulled her hand free of his, though she missed the warmth of his touch.

"I have to show you something," he said softly. "Will you take one more trip with me up the mountain?"

"Why should I?"

"There's no reason in the world you should," he admitted and pulled his foot out of the doorway. "But I'm asking you to anyway."

If he'd tried to smooth talk her into it, she might have refused. Instead, he'd played a new game. Honesty. And frankly, she was tired of fighting him. She knew she'd regret it later, of course, but at the moment, going with him was just easier.

The ride was tense, neither of them talking much. Colleen's mind was whirling with possibilities and questions. Why had he come? Where were they going? Why?

She sneaked glances at him, and he was always the same. Stoic. Eyes focused on the road ahead, which should have relieved her, since this drive could be treacherous. But she wished that he would glance her way. Give her some indication of what was going on. Instead, he drove the narrow, winding road up the mountain in silence, passing his ranch gates, and she turned in her seat to look at them as they drove by. "I thought we were going to your house."

"No," he said, not looking at her, focusing instead on the road stretched out in front of them.

Her stomach swirled uneasily as she realized where they were probably headed. The cabin. Where else would he be taking her on this mountain road? But then, why would he take her to the cabin? It was the first question she asked when he pulled into the drive and parked.

"Like I said at your house," he told her, climbing out of the huge SUV, "there's something I want to show you."

He took her hand, just as he had the first time, as they headed along the path to the cabin. But it was different now. The flower beds were weeded and bursting with newly planted, bright spring blossoms. Their scent rose up into the air and twisted with the ever-present aroma of pines.

The path itself was covered in fresh gravel. The surrounding pines had been trimmed back, still providing shade for the cabin but no longer threatening to tip over in a storm. The walls were painted a crisp white with navy blue trim around the windows. The chairs on the front porch had brand-new, dark blue cushions and there was a sturdy iron railing snaking along the porch, replacing the rotted wooden one that had snapped on their last visit.

It was beautiful. It was perfect. But she still couldn't buy it. "I can't," she said, looking up at him. "I can't buy this cabin, Sage. I appreciate you fixing it up for me but—"

"The cabin's not for sale anymore."

"What?"

"I bought it last week." He closed in on her and Colleen's heartbeat sped up. "Went to see Ed at his new place and paid him for it on the spot."

"Why?" she asked and was lucky she'd managed to squeeze out that single word.

"Let's go inside. There are some things I want to say to you."

She walked the path, ran her fingertips over the heavy black wrought-iron railing. When he noticed, he said, "I had my guys over here every day this week, fixing this place up. But the railing I installed myself." He caught her hand in his. "It's sturdy enough that you could do handstands on it, but I'd take it as a favor if you wouldn't. I don't want to risk losing you again."

Pleasure slid through her heart, leaving a trail of eager

anticipation in its wake. Was he saying what she thought he was? Could she believe? Her logical mind told her emotional half to get a grip, but it wasn't listening.

He smiled at her and tugged her along after him. "Come on."

She followed and the minute she stepped into the cabin, she realized he'd been at work here, too. The wood floors were gleaming under a fresh coat of wax. Bright throw rugs added splashes of color. Bookcases stood on either side of the wood-burning stove and there was a scent of lemon polish still hovering in the air.

"Linda, my housekeeper," Sage was saying as she walked through the little cabin that was now as shiny as new pennies. "She handled most of the inside work, though my guys did the paint job."

"It's beautiful," she told him, walking back to stop just a foot from him. "But I still don't understand. Why did you buy it?"

"For us," he said simply. He stood there opposite her in his black jeans, black leather jacket and white shirt and looked more gorgeous than she remembered. Just looking at the man gave her chills, but what he said next had every sense reeling.

"I bought it for us, Colleen. I wanted us to have this place to come to, just the two of us. I want us to always remember that we started here. That what's between us grew from here."

Oh, God. Her heartbeat was hammering so quickly now she could hardly draw a breath. But she didn't need air, Colleen realized. All she needed was to know that he meant this. Because if he had done all of this for the two of them, that could only mean that he loved her, and that would be everything.

"See," he said, moving toward her, laying both hands on her shoulders so that she could feel the strong, steady warmth of him seeping into her body. "I know now that I wasted what time I had with my father. I don't want to waste another minute of my time with you."

"Sage…"

"You said you loved me," he reminded her and gave her a slow smile. "I hope that hasn't changed, because I love you, too, Colleen."

Her eyes filled with tears and her breath caught in her throat. It was everything she'd hoped for. Only better.

"I love your mind. Your humor. Your kindness. I love everything about you."

"I can't believe this," she murmured, wondering if somehow she had fallen asleep back at the condo and maybe this was all just a very real, very involved dream.

"Believe it," he said, bending low enough to kiss her forehead before drawing back to look at her again. "Remember what J.D. said? Family is important and love is all that matters?"

"I remember." His eyes were shining down on her. The shutters were gone. They were clear and beautiful and glittering with emotions so deep they stole her breath.

"Well, *you're* my family. And my love for you is everything." He pulled her in close to him, lifted both hands and cupped her face between his palms. "I'm asking you to marry me, Colleen. Marry me and make a family of our own. Kids. Dogs. Horses. We'll have it all if you'll just say yes."

She wanted to. More than anything in her life, she wanted what he was offering. But she had to say, "I still want to get my practitioner's license. I want to have that rural practice I told you about."

He grinned and her heart nearly leaped up her throat. Would he always have this effect on her? God, she hoped so.

"Not a problem, honey," he said. "When you have calls to make, I'll watch the kids."

"Kids," she repeated, because she loved the sound of it.

"At least five or six."

She laughed then and felt her whole world come right again.

"So, will you marry me, Colleen?" He kissed the tip of her nose, then brushed her mouth with his. "Trust me, love. I've learned enough to listen. To know that though I could make it through my life alone, I don't want to. I want you—I *need* you—by my side. Always."

"There's really nowhere else I'd rather be," she said as she leaned into him. Her heart was full, and she had everything she'd ever dreamed of, right there offering her his heart. His life. His love. "Sage, I love you so much, of course I'll marry you."

"Thank God," he whispered and kissed her there in the room where they had first begun. Where they would come when they wanted to remember. When they wanted to celebrate the fact that love really was the only thing that mattered.

Epilogue

The wedding was two weeks later.

Colleen was amazed at just how quickly everything could come together. But Sage hadn't wanted to wait, and really, neither had she. Why wait when you had at last found the one person in the world for you?

Sage's ranch was decorated with flowers everywhere. He'd arranged for both a florist and a gardener to come in and turn the yard into a rainbow of color. There was also a hastily constructed dance floor on the wide front yard, lit by miles of tiny white twinkling lights that in the dusk looked like stars being born. Music from a local country band had the dance floor crowded and the scent of barbecue tempted everyone there.

It had been perfect, Colleen thought. Even the weather had cooperated, blessing the ceremony with a cool, clear day and a starry night.

She'd been on her feet for hours now, but she wasn't the least bit tired. Joy filled her, keeping a smile on her face and a thrill in her heart. She took a sip of champagne and looked out across the ranch at the people who had come to celebrate with them. It had been a small ceremony, only friends and family, and somehow that had made the whole thing more special.

Marlene was dancing with Walter Drake, the older woman laughing at something he said. Angie and Evan looked to be involved in a heated discussion, and Colleen frowned slightly. She could only hope that the situation would be cleared up soon, before it destroyed what the couple shared. Dylan was supervising the barbecue station and Chance was talking to Sage's ranch manager. Jenna and her husband were dancing and Colleen's mother and Aunt Donna were huddled at a table, no doubt planning their upcoming cruise.

"You're looking way too thoughtful for a bride," Sage said, coming up behind her. "And did I tell you how beautiful you are?"

She felt beautiful in her floor-length, off-the-shoulder white dress that skimmed her curves and swirled at her feet. But then, Sage was handsome in a black suit that was so elegantly cut he took her breath away.

"You did," she assured him, "but feel free to repeat yourself."

He chuckled, slid his arms around her middle and held her close to him. Colleen laid her hands on his arms and leaned her head back against his broad chest. "It's just such a perfect day."

He bent his head briefly to kiss her neck. "Any day I can get Colleen Falkner to say 'I do' is a good day."

She looked up at him. "That's Colleen Lassiter to you, mister."

He grinned and her heart did a flip. "Sounds good, doesn't it?"

"Sounds wonderful," she agreed, then nodded toward her mother and aunt. "They're so excited about the house you're having built for them on the ranch."

He laughed a little. "I know. Between the two of them, they're about to drive the architect wild enough to jump out a window."

Colleen's gaze slid across to the other side of the wide, manicured lawn, where the foundation of a house had already been laid. Sage had surprised her, and thrilled her mother, with his plans to build a three-bedroom house on the property for Laura and Donna. They would have their own place but be close enough to the main house that they could come and go as they pleased. The two women hadn't stopped talking about it since.

"They've changed the layout of the downstairs three times already," Sage mused, humor evident in his tone.

"You realize that with this beautiful house, they probably won't want to move to Florida after all?" And really, the two women had only decided on Florida because Aunt Donna already lived there and it would have been the easiest solution. Now things were different.

"Why would they, when Wyoming has everything?" he asked, then, smiling gently he added, "They only wanted to live together. Now they don't have to be in Florida to do it. And if your mom gets sick of winter, we'll buy the two of them a condo in Florida and they can go as often as they like."

Her heart did the flippy thing again as she realized

just what an amazing man she'd fallen in love with. "You're incredible."

"Not really," he said wryly, "but I'm glad you think so."

"I really do," she told him, turning in his arms so that she could look at him. Colleen knew that every ounce of love she felt for him had to be shining from her eyes, because she felt lit from within, as if she was absolutely glowing with the happiness she'd found.

"Besides," he said on a low laugh, "once the two of them have their passports in hand, I have a feeling they're going to be taking lots of trips. They can't wait for that cruise you're sending them on. But home will always be here. Waiting for them."

She studied his features, wanting to be absolutely sure he was okay with this and not just doing it because he knew she'd love having her family close by. "Are you really positive, Sage? There aren't many men willing to have their mother-in-law, not to mention her sister, living right on his doorstep."

All trace of amusement left his face as he met her eyes. He lifted one hand to smooth a stray lock of her hair back behind her ear before saying, "J.D.'s not here today—and damned if I don't wish he was. But I know what he'd say and I feel the same way. Family is important. Love is all that matters."

Tears filled her eyes. "Oh, you really know how to touch my heart."

"You are my heart, Colleen." He bent to kiss her gently, briefly. "And your mom. Donna. They're nice women. Why shouldn't they be with their family?" He grinned. "Besides, when our babies start arriving, how great will it be to have two willing babysitters close by?"

They'd already started trying to make their family, and Colleen sighed with the thought. Babies. A husband who loved her. Her vision still blurred with a wash of tears she was too happy to shed, she went up on her toes and kissed him. "I love you, Sage Lassiter."

"Damn straight you do," he said, his half grin taking all of the arrogance out of the statement.

"You're impossible."

"And very lucky," he added.

"Oh, that too," she agreed, sliding her arms around his waist and cuddling in close. He held her tightly enough that she heard the steady thump of his heart beneath her ear. Closing her eyes, she smiled to herself and relished the sensation of having her life be everything she could ever have hoped for.

A beautiful, love-filled wedding on a gorgeous ranch that was now her home. Her family was close and happy. Soon, she would be on her way to getting her practitioner's license and she had the love of her life holding her so gently it was as if she were a fragile, priceless treasure.

"So," he whispered, "how much longer do you figure we have to stay at this party?"

She smiled up at him. They would be spending their wedding night in the cabin where this had all begun. Tomorrow they were off by private jet for a week in Paris. And then home again to start their lives together. She couldn't wait. Colleen was as anxious as Sage to be alone with him.

"I love that we'll be at the cabin tonight," she told him.

"Me, too. And just think," he said, drawing her close for a hard squeeze, "one day, we'll take our grandkids out there, show them the railing and tell 'em about the day Grandma almost fell off the mountain—but how their strong, brave grandpa saved her, carried her inside and—"

Playfully, she slapped his chest. "We can't tell them *that*."

He caught her hand in his and kissed her palm. "How about we just tell them that Grandma saved Grandpa that day, too?"

Her heart melted. How was it possible to love a man as much as she loved Sage? And how had she ever lived without that love?

"How about we give the party one more hour?" she asked.

He groaned. "Deal. One hour, then if I don't have you, you'll be married to a dead man."

Colleen hugged him tight and turned her face up to his. "One hour. You can make it."

"For you," he promised, *"anything."*

Then he drew her onto the dance floor, and as their family and friends cheered, they danced their way into the future.

* * * * *